THE BIRDS CHRISTMAS CAROL

By

Kate Douglas Wiggin

The Bird's Christmas Carol

I

A LITTLE SNOW BIRD

It was very early Christmas morning, and in the stillness of the dawn, with the soft snow falling on the house-tops, a little child was born in the Bird household.

They had intended to name the baby Lucy, if it were a girl; but they had not expected her on Christmas morning, and a real Christmas baby was not to be lightly named—the whole family agreed in that.

They were consulting about it in the nursery. Mr. Bird said that he had assisted in naming the three boys, and that he should leave this matter entirely to Mrs. Bird; Donald wanted the child called "Dorothy," after a pretty, curly-haired girl who sat next him in school; Paul choose "Luella," for Luella was the nurse who had been with him during his whole babyhood, up to the time of his first trousers, and the name suggested all sorts of comfortable things. Uncle Jack said that the first girl should always be named for her mother, no matter how hideous the name happened to be.

Grandma said that she would prefer not to take any part in the discussion, and everybody suddenly remembered that Mrs. Bird had thought of naming the baby Lucy, for Grandma herself; and, while it would be indelicate for her to favor that name, it would be against human nature for her to suggest any other, under the circumstances.

Hugh, the "hitherto baby," if that is a possible term, sat in one corner and said nothing, but felt, in some mysterious way, that his nose was out of joint; for there was a newer baby now, a possibility he had never taken into consideration; and the "first girl," too,—a still higher development of treason, which made him actually green with jealousy.

But it was too profound a subject to be settled then and there, on the spot; besides, Mamma had not been asked, and everybody felt it rather absurd, after all, to forestall a decree that was certain to be absolutely wise, just, and perfect.

The reason that the subject had been brought up at all so early in the day lay in the fact that Mrs. Bird never allowed her babies to go over night unnamed. She was a person of so great decision of character that she would have blushed at such a thing; she said that to let blessed babies go dangling and dawdling about without names, for months and months, was enough to ruin them for life. She also said that if one could not make up one's mind in twenty-four hours it was a sign that—But I will not repeat the rest, as it might prejudice you against the most charming woman in the world.

So Donald took his new velocipede and went out to ride up and down the stone pavement and notch the shins of innocent people as they passed by, while Paul spun his musical top on the front steps.

But Hugh refused to leave the scene of action. He seated himself on the top stair in the hall, banged his head against the railing a few times, just by way of uncorking the vials of his wrath, and then subsided into gloomy silence, waiting to declare war if more "first girl babies" were thrust upon a family already surfeited with that unnecessary article.

Meanwhile dear Mrs. Bird lay in her room, weak, but safe and happy, with her sweet girl baby by her side and the heaven of motherhood opening again before her. Nurse was making gruel in the kitchen, and the room was dim and quiet. There was a cheerful open fire in the grate, but though the shutters were closed, the side windows that looked out on the Church of Our Saviour, next door, were a little open.

Suddenly a sound of music poured out into the bright air and drifted into the chamber. It was the boy choir singing Christmas anthems. Higher and higher rose the clear, fresh voices, full of hope and cheer, as children's voices always are. Fuller and fuller grew the burst of melody as one glad strain fell upon another in joyful harmony:—

"Carol, brothers, carol,Carol joyfully,Carol the good tidings,Carol merrily!And pray a gladsome ChristmasFor all your fellow-men:Carol, brothers, carol,Christmas Day again."

One verse followed another, always with the same sweet refrain:—

"And pray a gladsome ChristmasFor all your fellow-men:Carol, brothers, carol,Christmas Day again."

Mrs. Bird thought, as the music floated in upon her gentle sleep, that she had slipped into heaven with her new baby, and that the angels were bidding them welcome. But the tiny bundle by her side stirred a little, and though it was scarcely more than the ruffling of a feather, she awoke; for the mother-ear is so close to the heart that it can hear the faintest whisper of a child.

She opened her eyes and drew the baby closer. It looked like a rose dipped in milk, she thought, this pink and white blossom of girlhood, or like a pink cherub, with its halo of pale yellow hair, finer than floss silk.

"Carol, brothers, carol,Carol joyfully,Carol the good tidings,Carol merrily!"

The voices were brimming over with joy.

"Why, my baby," whispered Mrs. Bird in soft surprise, "I had forgotten what day it was. You are a little Christmas child, and we will name you 'Carol'—mother's Christmas Carol!"

"What!" said Mr. Bird, coming in softly and closing the door behind him.

"Why, Donald, don't you think 'Carol' is a sweet name for a Christmas baby? It came to me just a moment ago in the singing, as I was lying here half asleep and half awake."

"I think it is a charming name, dear heart, and sounds just like you, and I hope that, being a girl, this baby has some chance of being as lovely as her mother;"—at which speech from the baby's papa Mrs. Bird, though she was as weak and tired as she could be, blushed with happiness.

And so Carol came by her name.

Of course, it was thought foolish by many people, though Uncle Jack declared laughingly that it was very strange if a whole family of Birds could not be indulged in a single Carol; and Grandma, who adored the child, thought the name much more appropriate than Lucy, but was glad that people would probably think it short for Caroline.

Perhaps because she was born in holiday time, Carol was a very happy baby. Of course, she was too tiny to understand the joy of Christmas-tide, but people say there is everything in a good beginning, and she may have breathed in unconsciously the fragrance of evergreens and holiday dinners; while the peals of sleigh-bells and the laughter of happy children may have fallen upon her baby ears and wakened in them a glad surprise at the merry world she had come to live in.

Her cheeks and lips were as red as holly-berries; her hair was for all the world the color of a Christmas candle-flame; her eyes were bright as stars; her laugh like a chime of Christmas-bells, and her tiny hands forever outstretched in giving.

"SHE IS A LITTLE CHRISTMAS CHILD"

Such a generous little creature you never saw! A spoonful of bread and milk had always to be taken by Mamma or nurse before Carol could enjoy her supper; whatever bit of cake or sweetmeat found its way into her pretty fingers was straightway broken in half to be shared with Donald, Paul, or Hugh; and when they made believe nibble the morsel with affected enjoyment, she would clap her hands and crow with delight.

"Why does she do it?" asked Donald thoughtfully. "None of us boys ever did."

"I hardly know," said Mamma, catching her darling to her heart, "except that she is a little Christmas child, and so she has a tiny share of the blessedest birthday the world ever knew!"

II

DROOPING WINGS

it was December, ten years later.

Carol had seen nine Christmas trees lighted on her birthdays, one after another; nine times she had assisted in the holiday festivities of the household, though in her babyhood her share of the gayeties was somewhat limited.

For five years, certainly, she had hidden presents for Mamma and Papa in their own bureau drawers, and harbored a number of secrets sufficiently large to burst a baby brain, had it not been for the relief gained by whispering them all to Mamma, at night, when she was in her crib, a proceeding which did not in the least lessen the value of a secret in her innocent mind.

For five years she had heard "'Twas the night before Christmas," and hung up a scarlet stocking many sizes too large for her, and pinned a sprig of holly on her little white nightgown, to show Santa Claus that she was a "truly" Christmas child, and dreamed of fur-coated saints and toy-packs and reindeer, and wished everybody a "Merry Christmas" before it was light in the morning, and lent every one of her new toys to the neighbors' children before noon, and eaten turkey and plum-pudding, and gone to bed at night in a trance of happiness at the day's pleasures.

Donald was away at college now. Paul and Hugh were great manly fellows, taller than their mother. Papa Bird had gray hairs in his whiskers; and Grandma, God bless her, had been four Christmases in heaven.

But Christmas in the Birds' Nest was scarcely as merry now as it used to be in the bygone years, for the little child, that once brought such an added blessing to the day, lay month after month a patient, helpless invalid, in the room where she was born. She had never been very strong in body, and it was with a pang of terror her mother and father noticed, soon after she was five years old, that she began to limp, ever so slightly; to complain too often of weariness, and to nestle close to her mother, saying she "would rather not go out to play, please." The illness was slight at first, and hope was always stirring in Mrs. Bird's heart. "Carol would feel stronger in the summer-time;" or, "She would be better when she had spent a year in the country;" or, "She would outgrow it;" or, "They would try a new physician;" but by and by it came to be all too sure that no physician save One could make Carol strong again, and that no "summer-time" nor "country air," unless it were the everlasting summer-time in a heavenly country, could bring back the little girl to health.

The cheeks and lips that were once as red as holly-berries faded to faint pink; the star-like eyes grew softer, for they often gleamed through tears; and the gay child-laugh, that had been like a chime of Christmas bells, gave place to a smile so lovely, so touching, so tender and patient, that it filled every corner of the house with a gentle radiance that might have come from the face of the Christ-child himself.

Love could do nothing; and when we have said that we have said all, for it is stronger than anything else in the whole wide world. Mr. and Mrs. Bird were talking it over one evening, when all the children were asleep. A famous physician had visited them that day, and told them that some time, it might be in one year, it might be in more, Carol would slip quietly off into heaven, whence she came.

"It is no use to close our eyes to it any longer," said Mr. Bird, as he paced up and down the library floor; "Carol will never be well again. It almost seems as if I could not bear it when I think of that loveliest child doomed to lie there day after day, and, what is still more, to suffer pain that we are helpless to keep away from her. Merry Christmas, indeed; it gets to be the saddest day in the year to me!" and poor Mr. Bird sank into a chair by the table, and buried his face in his hands to keep his wife from seeing the tears that would come in spite of all his efforts.

"But, Donald, dear," said sweet Mrs. Bird, with trembling voice, "Christmas Day may not be so merry with us as it used, but it is very happy, and that is better, and very blessed, and that is better yet. I suffer chiefly for Carol's sake, but I have almost given up being sorrowful for my own. I am too happy in the child, and I see too clearly what she has done for us and the other children. Donald and Paul and Hugh were three strong, willful, boisterous boys, but now you seldom see such tenderness, devotion, thought for others, and self-denial in lads of their years. A quarrel or a hot word is almost unknown in this house, and why? Carol would hear it, and it would distress her, she is so full of love and goodness. The boys study with all their might and main. Why? Partly, at least, because they like to teach Carol, and amuse her by telling her what they read. When the seamstress comes, she likes to sew in Miss Carol's room, because there she forgets her own troubles, which, Heaven knows, are sore enough! And as for me, Donald, I am a better woman every day for Carol's sake; I have to be her eyes, ears, feet, hands,—her strength, her hope; and she, my own little child, is my example!"

"I was wrong, dear heart," said Mr. Bird more cheerfully; "we will try not to repine, but to rejoice instead, that we have an 'angel of the house.'"

"And as for her future," Mrs. Bird went on, "I think we need not be over-anxious. I feel as if she did not belong altogether to us, but that when she has done what God sent her for, He will take her back to Himself—and it may not be very long!" Here it was poor Mrs. Bird's turn to break down, and Mr. Bird's turn to comfort her.

III

THE BIRDS' NEST

carol herself knew nothing of motherly tears and fatherly anxieties; she lived on peacefully in the room where she was born.

But you never would have known that room; for Mr. Bird had a great deal of money, and though he felt sometimes as if he wanted to throw it all in the sea, since it could not buy a strong body for his little girl, yet he was glad to make the place she lived in just as beautiful as it could be.

The room had been extended by the building of a large addition that hung out over the garden below, and was so filled with windows that it might have been a conservatory. The ones on the side were thus still nearer the Church of Our Saviour than they used to be; those in front looked out on the beautiful harbor, and those in the back commanded a view of nothing in particular but a narrow alley; nevertheless, they were pleasantest of all to Carol, for the Ruggles family lived in the alley, and the nine little, middle-sized, and big Ruggles children were a source of inexhaustible interest.

The shutters could all be opened and Carol could take a real sun-bath in this lovely glass house, or they could all be closed when the dear head ached or the dear eyes were tired. The carpet was of soft gray, with clusters of green bay and holly leaves. The furniture was of white wood, on which an artist had painted snow scenes and Christmas trees and groups of merry children ringing bells and singing carols.

Donald had made a pretty, polished shelf, and screwed it on the outside of the foot-board, and the boys always kept this full of blooming plants, which they changed from time to time; the head-board, too, had a bracket on either side, where there were pots of maiden-hair ferns.

Love-birds and canaries hung in their golden houses in the windows, and they, poor caged things, could hop as far from their wooden perches as Carol could venture from her little white bed.

On one side of the room was a bookcase filled with hundreds—yes, I mean it—with hundreds and hundreds of books; books with gay-colored pictures, books without; books with black and white outline sketchcs, books with none at all; books with verses, books with stories; books that made children laugh, and some, only a few, that made them cry; books with words of one syllable for tiny boys and girls, and books with words of fearful length to puzzle wise ones.

This was Carol's "Circulating Library." Every Saturday she chose ten books, jotting their names down in a diary; into these she slipped cards that said:—

"Please keep this book two weeks and read it.

With love, CAROL BIRD."

Then Mrs. Bird stepped into her carriage and took the ten books to the Children's Hospital, and brought home ten others that she had left there the fortnight before.

This was a source of great happiness; for some of the Hospital children that were old enough to print or write, and were strong enough to do it, wrote Carol sweet little letters about the books, and she answered them, and they grew to be friends. (It is very funny, but you do not always have to see people to love them. Just think about it, and tell me if it isn't so.)

There was a high wainscoting of wood about the room, and on top of this, in a narrow gilt framework, ran a row of illuminated pictures, illustrating fairy tales, all in dull blue and gold and scarlet and silver. From the door to the closet there was the story of "The Fair One with Golden Locks;" from closet to bookcase, ran "Puss in Boots;" from bookcase to fireplace, was "Jack the Giant-killer;" and on the other side of the room were "Hop o' my Thumb," "The Sleeping Beauty," and "Cinderella."

Then there was a great closet full of beautiful things to wear, but they were all dressing-gowns and slippers and shawls; and there were drawers full of toys and games, but they were such as you could play with on your lap. There were no ninepins, nor balls, nor bows and arrows, nor bean bags, nor tennis rackets; but, after all, other children needed these more than Carol Bird, for she was always happy and contented, whatever she had or whatever she lacked; and after the room had been made so lovely for her, on her eighth Christmas, she always called herself, in fun, a "Bird of Paradise."

On these particular December days she was happier than usual, for Uncle Jack was coming from England to spend the holidays. Dear, funny, jolly, loving, wise Uncle Jack, who came every two or three years, and brought so much joy with him that the world looked as black as a thunder-cloud for a week after he went away again.

The mail had brought this letter:—

LONDON, NOVEMBER , -.

Wish you merry Christmas, you dearest birdlings in America! Preen your feathers, and stretch the Birds' nest a trifle, if you please, and let Uncle Jack in for the holidays. I am coming with such a trunk full of treasures that you'll have to borrow the stockings of Barnum's Giant and Giantess; I am coming to squeeze a certain little lady-bird until she cries for mercy; I am coming to see if I can find a boy to take care of a black pony that I bought lately. It's the strangest thing I ever knew; I've hunted all over Europe, and can't find a boy to suit me! I'll tell you why. I've set my heart on finding one with a dimple in his chin, because this pony particularly likes dimples! "Hurrah!" cried Hugh; "bless my dear dimple; I'll never be ashamed of it again."

Please drop a note to the clerk of the weather, and have a good, rousing snow-storm—say on the twenty-second. None of your meek, gentle, nonsensical, shilly-shallying snow-storms; not the sort where the flakes float lazily down from the sky as if they didn't care whether they ever got here or not and then melt away as soon as they touch the earth, but a regular business-like whizzing, whirring, blurring, cutting snow-storm, warranted to freeze and stay on!

I should like rather a LARGE Christmas tree, if it's convenient: not one of those "sprigs," five or six feet high, that you used to have three or four years ago, when the birdlings were not fairly feathered out; but a tree of some size. Set it up in the garret, if necessary, and then we can cut a hole in the roof if the tree chances to be too high for the room.

Tell Bridget to begin to fatten a turkey. Tell her that by the twentieth of December that turkey must not be able to stand on its legs for fat, and then on the next three days she must allow it to recline easily on its side, and stuff it to bursting. (One ounce of stuffing beforehand is worth a pound afterwards.)

The pudding must bc unusually huge, and darkly, deeply, lugubriously blue in color. It must be stuck so full of plums that the pudding itself will ooze out into the pan and not be brought on to the table at all. I expect to be there by the twentieth, to manage these little things myself,—remembering it is the early Bird that catches the worm,—but give you the instructions in case I should be delayed.

And Carol must decide on the size of the tree—she knows best, she was a Christmas child; and she must plead for the snow-storm—the "clerk of the weather" may pay some attention to her; and she must look up the boy with the dimple for me—she's likelier to find him than I am, this minute. She must advise about the turkey, and Bridget must bring the pudding to her bedside and let her drop every separate plum into it and stir it once for luck, or I'll not eat a single slice—for Carol is the dearest part of Christmas to Uncle Jack, and he'll have none of it without her. She is better than all the turkeys and puddings and apples and spare-ribs and wreaths and garlands and mistletoe and stockings and chimneys and sleigh-bells in Christendom! She is the very sweetest Christmas Carol that was ever written, said, sung, or chanted, and I am coming as fast as ships and railway trains can carry me, to tell her so.

Carol's joy knew no bounds. Mr. and Mrs. Bird laughed like children and kissed each other for sheer delight, and when the boys heard it they simply whooped like wild Indians; until the Ruggles family, whose back yard joined their garden, gathered at the door and wondered what was "up" in the big house.

CAROL AT HER WINDOW

IV

"BIRDS OF A FEATHER FLOCK TOGETHER"

uncle Jack did really come on the twentieth. He was not detained by business, nor did he get left behind nor snowed up, as frequently happens in stories, and in real life too, I am afraid. The snow-storm came also; and the turkey nearly died a natural and premature death from overeating. Donald came, too; Donald, with a line of down upon his upper lip, and Greek and Latin on his tongue, and stores of knowledge in his handsome head, and stories—bless me, you couldn't turn over a chip without reminding Donald of something that happened "at College." One or the other was always at Carol's bedside, for they fancied her paler than she used to be, and they could not bear her out of sight. It was Uncle Jack, though, who sat beside her in the winter twilights. The room was quiet, and almost dark, save for the snow-light outside, and the flickering flame of the fire, that danced over the "Sleeping Beauty's" face and touched the Fair One's golden locks with ruddier glory. Carol's hand (all too thin and white these latter days) lay close clasped in Uncle Jack's, and they talked together quietly of many, many things.

"I want to tell you all about my plans for Christmas this year, Uncle Jack," said Carol, on the first evening of his visit, "because it will be the loveliest one I ever had. The boys laugh at me for caring so much about it; but it isn't altogether because it is Christmas, nor because it is my birthday; but long, long ago, when I first began to be ill, I used to think, the first thing when I waked on Christmas morning, 'To-day is Christ's birthday—*and mine*!' I did not put the words close together, you know, because that made it seem too bold; but I first said, 'Christ's birthday,' out loud, and then, in a minute, softly to myself—'*and mine*!' 'Christ's birthday—*and mine*!' And so I do not quite feel about Christmas as other girls do. Mamma says she supposes that ever so many other children have been born on that day. I often wonder where they are, Uncle Jack, and whether it is a dear thought to them, too, or whether I am so much in bed, and so often alone, that it means more to me. Oh, I do hope that none of them are poor, or cold, or hungry; and I wish—I wish they were all as happy as I, because they are really my little brothers and sisters. Now, Uncle Jack dear, I am going to try and make somebody happy every single Christmas that I live, and this year it is to be the 'Ruggleses in the rear.'"

"That large and interesting brood of children in the little house at the end of the back garden?"

"Yes; isn't it nice to see so many together?—and, Uncle Jack, why do the big families always live in the small houses, and the small families in the big houses? We ought to call them the Ruggles children, of course; but Donald began talking of them as the 'Ruggleses in the rear,' and Papa and Mamma took it up, and now we cannot seem to help it. The house was built for Mr. Carter's coachman, but Mr. Carter lives in Europe, and the gentleman who rents his place for him doesn't care what happens to it, and so this poor family came to live there. When they first moved in, I used to sit in my window and watch them play in their back yard; they are so strong, and jolly, and good-natured;—and then, one day, I had a terrible headache, and Donald asked them if they would please not scream quite so loud, and they explained that they were having a game of circus, but that they would change and play 'Deaf and Dumb Asylum' all the afternoon."

"Ha, ha, ha!" laughed Uncle Jack, "what an obliging family, to be sure!"

"Yes, we all thought it very funny, and I smiled at them from the window when I was well enough to be up again. Now, Sarah Maud comes to her door when the children come home from school, and if Mamma nods her head, 'Yes,' that means 'Carol is very well,' and then you ought to hear the little Ruggleses yell,—I believe they try to see how much noise they can make; but if Mamma shakes her head, 'No,' they always play at quiet games. Then, one day, 'Cary,' my pet canary, flew out of her cage, and Peter Ruggles caught her and brought her back, and I had him up here in my room to thank him."

"Is Peter the oldest?"

"No; Sarah Maud is the oldest—she helps do the washing; and Peter is the next. He is a dress-maker's boy."

"And which is the pretty little red-haired girl?"

"That's Kitty."

"And the fat youngster?"

"Baby Larry."

"And that—most freckled one?"

"Now, don't laugh—that's Peoria."

"Carol, you are joking."

"No, really, Uncle dear. She was born in Peoria; that's all."

"And is the next boy Oshkosh?"

"No," laughed Carol, "the others are Susan, and Clement, and Eily, and Cornelius; they all look exactly alike, except that some of them have more freckles than the others."

"How did you ever learn all their names?"

"Why, I have what I call a 'window-school.' It is too cold now; but in warm weather I am wheeled out on my balcony, and the Ruggleses climb up and walk along our garden fence, and sit down on the roof of our carriage-house. That brings them quite near, and I tell them stories. On Thanksgiving Day they came up for a few minutes,—it was quite warm at eleven o'clock,—and we told each other what we had to be thankful for; but they gave such queer answers that Papa had to run away for fear of laughing; and I couldn't understand them very well. Susan was thankful for '*trunks*,' of all things in the world; Cornelius, for 'horse-cars;' Kitty, for 'pork steak;' while Clem, who is very quiet, brightened up when I came to him, and said he was thankful for '*his lame puppy*.' Wasn't that pretty?"

"It might teach some of us a lesson, mightn't it, little girl?"

"That's what Mamma said. Now I'm going to give this whole Christmas to the Ruggleses; and, Uncle Jack, I earned part of the money myself."

"You, my bird; how?"

"Well, you see, it could not be my own, own Christmas if Papa gave me all the money, and I thought to really keep Christ's birthday I ought to do something of my very own; and so I talked with Mamma. Of course she thought of something lovely; she always does: Mamma's head is just brimming over with lovely thoughts,—all I have to do is ask, and out pops the very one I want. This thought was to let her write down, just as I told her, a description of how a child lived in her own room for three years, and what she did to amuse herself; and we sent it to a magazine and got twenty-five dollars for it. Just think!"

"Well, well," cried Uncle Jack, "my little girl a real author! And what are you going to do with this wonderful 'own' money of yours?"

"I shall give the nine Ruggleses a grand Christmas dinner here in this very room—that will be Papa's contribution,—and afterwards a beautiful Christmas tree, fairly blooming with presents—that will be my part; for I have another way of adding to my twenty-five dollars, so that I can buy nearly anything I choose. I should like it very much if you would sit at the head of the table, Uncle Jack, for nobody could ever be frightened of you, you dearest, dearest, dearest thing that ever was! Mamma is going to help us, but Papa and the boys are going to eat together downstairs for fear of making the little Ruggleses shy; and after we've had a merry time with the tree we can open my window and all listen together to the music at the evening church-service, if it comes before the children go. I have written a letter to the organist, and asked him if I might have the two songs I like best. Will you see if it is all right?"

BIRDS' NEST, December , -.

DEAR MR. WILKIE,—I am the little girl who lives next door to the church, and, as I seldom go out, the music on practice days and Sundays is one of my greatest pleasures.

I want to know if you can have "Carol, brothers, carol," on Christmas night, and if the boy who sings "My ain countree" so beautifully may please sing that too. I think it is the loveliest thing in the world, but it always makes me cry; doesn't it you?

If it isn't too much trouble, I hope they can sing them both quite early, as after ten o'clock I may be asleep.

Yours respectfully,

CAROL BIRD.

P.S.—The reason I like "Carol, brothers, carol," is because the choir-boys sang it eleven years ago, the morn ing I was born, and put it into Mamma's head to call me Carol. She didn't remember then that my other name would be Bird, because she was half asleep, and could only think of one thing at a time. Donald says if I had been born on the Fourth of July they would have named me "Independence," or if on the twenty-second of February, "Georgina," or even "Cherry," like Cherry in "Martin Chuzzlewit;" but I like my own name and birthday best.

Yours truly,

CAROL BIRD.

Uncle Jack thought the letter quite right, and did not even smile at her telling the organist so many family items.

The days flew by as they always fly in holiday time, and it was Christmas Eve before anybody knew it. The family festival was quiet and very pleasant, but almost overshadowed by the grander preparations for the next day. Carol and Elfrida, her pretty German nurse, had ransacked books, and introduced so many plans, and plays, and customs, and merry-makings from Germany, and Holland, and England, and a dozen other countries, that you would scarcely have known how or where you were keeping Christmas. Even the dog and the cat had enjoyed their celebration under Carol's direction. Each had a tiny table with a lighted candle in the centre, and a bit of Bologna sausage placed very near it; and everybody laughed till the tears stood in their eyes to see Villikins and Dinah struggle to nibble the sausages, and at the same time to evade the candle flame. Villikins barked, and sniffed, and howled in impatience, and after many vain attempts succeeded in dragging off the prize, though he singed his nose in doing it. Dinah, meanwhile, watched him placidly, her delicate nostrils quivering with expectation, and, after all the excitement had subsided, walked with dignity to the table, her beautiful gray satin trail sweeping behind her, and, calmly putting up one velvet paw, drew the sausage gently down, and walked out of the room without turning a hair, so to speak. Elfrida had scattered handfuls of seed over the snow in the garden, that the wild birds might have a comfortable breakfast next morning, and had stuffed bundles of dry grasses in the fireplaces, so that the reindeer of Santa Claus could refresh themselves after their long gallops across country. This was really only done for fun, but it pleased Carol.

And when, after dinner, the whole family had gone to the church to see the Christmas decorations, Carol limped out on her slender crutches, and with Elfrida's help, placed all the family boots in a row in the upper hall. That was to keep the dear ones from quarreling all through the year. There were Papa's stout top boots; Mamma's pretty buttoned shoes next; then Uncle Jack's, Donald's, Paul's, and Hugh's; and at the end of the line her own little white worsted slippers. Last, and sweetest of all, like the children in Austria, she put a lighted candle in her window to guide the dear Christ-child, lest he should stumble in the dark night as he passed up the deserted street. This done, she dropped into bed, a rather tired, but very happy Christmas fairy.

V

SOME OTHER BIRDS ARE TAUGHT TO FLY

Before the earliest Ruggles could wake and toot his five-cent tin horn, Mrs. Ruggles was up and stirring about the house, for it was a gala day in the family. Gala day! I should think so! Were not her nine "childern" invited to a dinner-party at the great house, and weren't they going to sit down free and equal with the mightiest in the land? She had been preparing for this grand occasion ever since the receipt of Carol Bird's invitation, which, by the way, had been speedily enshrined in an old photograph frame and hung under the looking-glass in the most prominent place in the kitchen, where it stared the occasional visitor directly in the eye, and made him livid with envy:—

BIRDS' NEST, December , -.

DEAR MRS. RUGGLES,—I am going to have a dinner-party on Christmas Day, and would like to have all your children come. I want them every one, please, from Sarah Maud to Baby Larry. Mamma says dinner will be at half past five, and the Christmas tree at seven; so you may expect them home at nine o'clock. Wishing you a Merry Christmas and a Happy New Year, I am

Yours truly,

CAROL BIRD.

Breakfast was on the table promptly at seven o'clock, and there was very little of it, too; for it was an excellent day for short rations, though Mrs. Ruggles heaved a sigh as she reflected that the boys, with their India-rubber stomachs, would be just as hungry the day after the dinner-party as if they had never had any at all.

As soon as the scanty meal was over, she announced the plan of the campaign: "Now, Susan, you an' Kitty wash up the dishes; an' Peter, can't yer spread up the beds, so't I can git ter cuttin' out Larry's new suit? I ain't satisfied with his clo'es, an' I thought in the night of a way to make him a dress out o' my old red plaid shawl—kind o' Scotch style, yer know, with the fringe 't the bottom.—Eily, you go find the comb and take the snarls out the fringe, that's a lady! You little young ones clear out from under foot! Clem, you and Con hop into bed with Larry while I wash yer underflannins; 'twon't take long to dry 'em.—Yes, I know it's bothersome, buy yer can't go int' s'ciety 'thout takin' some trouble, 'n' anyhow I couldn't git round to 'em last night.—Sarah Maud, I think 'twould be perfeckly han'som' if you ripped them brass buttons off yer uncle's *po*liceman's coat 'n' sewed 'em in a row up the front o' yer green skirt. Susan, you must iron out yours 'n' Kitty's apurns; 'n' there, I come mighty near forgettin' Peory's stockin's! I counted the whole lot last night when I was washin' of 'em, 'n' there ain't but nineteen anyhow yer fix 'em, 'n' no nine pairs mates nohow; 'n' I ain't goin' ter have my childern wear odd stockin's to a dinner-comp'ny, fetched up as I was!—Eily, can't you run out and ask Mis' Cullen ter lend me a pair o' stockin's for Peory, 'n' tell her if she will, Peory'll give Jim half her candy when she gets home. Won't yer, Peory?"

Peoria was young and greedy, and thought the remedy so out of all proportion to the disease, that she set up a deafening howl at the projected bargain—a howl so rebellious and so entirely out of season that her mother started in her direction with flashing eye and uplifted hand; but she let it fall suddenly, saying, "No, I vow I won't lick ye Christmas Day, if yer drive me crazy; but speak up smart, now, 'n' say whether yer'd ruther give Jim Cullen half yer candy or go bare-legged ter the party?" The matter being put so plainly, Peoria collected her faculties, dried her tears, and chose the lesser evil, Clem having hastened the decision by an affectionate wink, that meant he'd go halves with her on his candy.

"That's a lady!" cried her mother. "Now, you young ones that ain't doin' nothin', play all yer want ter before noontime, for after ye git through eatin' at twelve o'clock me 'n' Sarah Maud's goin' ter give yer sech a washin' 'n' combin' 'n' dressin' as yer never had before 'n' never will agin likely, 'n' then I'm goin' to set yer down 'n' give yer two solid hours trainin' in manners; 'n' 'twon't be no foolin' neither."

"All we've got ter do's go eat!" grumbled Peter.

"Well, that's enough," responded his mother; "there's more'n one way of eatin', let me tell yer, 'n' you've got a heap ter learn about it, Peter Ruggles. Land sakes, I wish you childern could see the way I was fetched up to eat. I never took a meal o' vittles in the kitchen before I married Ruggles; but yer can't keep up that style with nine young ones 'n' yer Pa always off ter sea."

The big Ruggleses worked so well, and the little Ruggleses kept from "under foot" so successfully, that by one o'clock nine complete toilets were laid out in solemn grandeur on the beds. I say, "complete;" but I do not know whether they would be called so in the best society. The law of compensation had been well applied: he that had necktie had no cuffs; she that had sash had no handkerchief, and *vice versa*; but they all had shoes and a certain amount of clothing, such as it was, the outside layer being in every case quite above criticism.

"Now, Sarah Maud," said Mrs. Ruggles, her face shining with excitement, "everything's red up an' we can begin. I've got a boiler 'n' a kettle 'n' a pot o' hot water. Peter, you go into the back bedroom, 'n' I'll take Susan, Kitty, Peory, 'n' Cornelius; 'n' Sarah Maud, you take Clem, 'n' Eily, 'n' Larry, one to a time. Scrub 'em 'n' rinse 'em, or 't any rate git's fur's yer can with 'em, and then I'll finish 'em off while you do yerself."

Sarah Maud couldn't have scrubbed with any more decision and force if she had been doing floors, and the little Ruggleses bore it bravely, not from natural heroism, but for the joy that was set before them. Not being satisfied, however, with the "tone" of their complexions, and feeling that the number of freckles to the square inch was too many to be tolerated in the highest social circles, she wound up operations by applying a little Bristol brick from the knife-board, which served as the proverbial "last straw," from under which the little Ruggleses issued rather red and raw and out of temper. When the clock struck four they were all clothed, and most of them in their right minds, ready for those last touches that always take the most time.

Kitty's red hair was curled in thirty-four ringlets, Sarah Maud's was braided in one pig-tail, and Susan's and Eily's in two braids apiece, while Peoria's resisted all advances in the shape of hair oils and stuck out straight on all sides, like that of the Circassian girl of the circus—so Clem said; and he was sent into the bedroom for it, too, from whence he was dragged out forgivingly, by Peoria herself, five minutes later. Then, exciting moment, came linen collars for some and neckties and bows for others,—a magnificent green glass breastpin was sewed into Peter's purple necktie,—and Eureka! the Ruggleses were dressed, and Solomon in all his glory was not arrayed like one of these!

A row of seats was then formed directly through the middle of the kitchen. Of course, there were not quite chairs enough for ten, since the family had rarely wanted to sit down all at once, somebody always being out or in bed, or otherwise en gaged, but the wood-box and the coal-hod finished out the line nicely, and nobody thought of grumbling. The children took their places according to age, Sarah Maud at the head and Larry on the coal-hod, and Mrs. Ruggles seated herself in front, surveying them proudly as she wiped the sweat of honest toil from her brow.

"Well," she exclaimed, "if I do say so as shouldn't, I never see a cleaner, more stylish mess o' childern in my life! I do wish Ruggles could look at ye for a minute!—Larry Ruggles, how many times have I got ter tell yer not ter keep pullin' at yer sash? Haven't I told yer if it comes ontied, yer waist 'n' skirt'll part comp'ny in the middle, 'n' then where'll yer be?—Now look me in the eye, all of yer! I've of'en told yer what kind of a family the McGrills was. I've got reason to be proud, goodness knows! Your uncle is on the *po*lice force o' New York city; you can take up the paper most any day an' see his name printed right out—James McGrill,—'n' I can't have my children fetched up common, like some folks'; when they go out they've got to have clo'es, and learn to act decent! Now I want ter see how yer goin' to behave when yer git there to-night. 'Tain't so awful easy as you think 'tis. Let's start in at the beginnin' 'n' act out the whole business.

"I WANT TER SEE HOW YER GOIN' TER BEHAVE"

Pile into the bedroom, there, every last one o' ye, 'n' show me how yer goin' to go int' the parlor. This'll be the parlor, 'n' I'll be Mis' Bird."

The youngsters hustled into the next room in high glee, and Mrs. Ruggles drew herself up in the chair with an infinitely haughty and purse-proud expression that much better suited a descendant of the McGrills than modest Mrs. Bird.

The bedroom was small, and there presently ensued such a clatter that you would have thought a herd of wild cattle had broken loose. The door opened, and they straggled in, all the younger ones giggling, with Sarah Maud at the head, looking as if she had been caught in the act of stealing sheep; while Larry, being last in line, seemed to think the door a sort of gate of heaven which would be shut in his face if he didn't get there in time; accordingly he struggled ahead of his elders and disgraced himself by tumbling in head foremost.

Mrs. Ruggles looked severe. "There, I knew yer'd do it in some sech fool way! Now go in there and try it over again, every last one o' ye, 'n' if Larry can't come in on two legs he can stay ter home,—d' yer hear?"

The matter began to assume a graver aspect; the little Ruggleses stopped giggling and backed into the bedroom, issuing presently with lock step, Indian file, a scared and hunted expression on every countenance.

"No, no, no!" cried Mrs. Ruggles, in despair. "That's worse yet; yer look for all the world like a gang o' pris'ners! There ain't no style ter that: spread out more, can't yer, 'n' act kind o' careless-like—nobody's goin' ter kill ye! That ain't what a dinner-party is!"

The third time brought deserved success, and the pupils took their seats in the row. "Now, yer know," said Mrs. Ruggles impressively, "there ain't enough decent hats to go round, 'n' if there was I don' know's I'd let yer wear 'em, for the boys would never think to take 'em off when they got inside, for they never do—but anyhow, there ain't enough good ones. Now, look me in the eye. You're only goin' jest round the corner; you needn't wear no hats, none of yer, 'n' when yer get int' the parlor, 'n' they ask yer ter lay off yer hats, Sarah Maud must speak up 'n' say it was sech a pleasant evenin' 'n' sech a short walk that yer left yer hats to home. Now, can yer remember?"

All the little Ruggleses shouted, "Yes, marm!" in chorus.

"What have *you* got ter do with it?" demanded their mother; "did I tell *you* to say it? Warn't I talkin' ter Sarah Maud?"

The little Ruggleses hung their diminished heads. "Yes, marm," they piped, more discreetly.

"Now we won't leave nothin' to chance; git up, all of ye, an' try it.—Speak up, Sarah Maud."

Sarah Maud's tongue clove to the roof of her mouth.

"Quick!"

"Ma thought—it was—sech a pleasant hat that we'd—we'd better leave our short walk to home," recited Sarah Maud, in an agony of mental effort.

This was too much for the boys. An earthquake of suppressed giggles swept all along the line.

"Oh, whatever shall I do with yer?" moaned the unhappy mother; "I s'pose I've got to learn it to yer!"—which she did, word for word, until Sarah Maud thought she could stand on her head and say it backwards.

"Now, Cornelius, what are *you* goin' ter say ter make yerself good comp'ny?"

"Do? Me? Dunno!" said Cornelius, turning pale, with unexpected responsibility.

"Well, ye ain't goin' to set there like a bump on a log 'thout sayin' a word ter pay for yer vittles, air ye? Ask Mis' Bird how she's feelin' this evenin', or if Mr. Bird's hevin' a busy season, or how this kind o' weather agrees with him, or somethin' like that.—Now we'll make b'lieve we've got ter the dinner—that won't be so hard, 'cause yer'll have somethin' to do—it's awful bothersome to stan' round an' act stylish.—If they have napkins, Sarah Maud down to Peory may put 'em in their laps, 'n' the rest of ye can tuck 'em in yer necks. Don't eat with yer fingers—don't grab no vittles off one 'nother's plates; don't reach out for nothin', but wait till yer asked, 'n' if you never *git* asked don't git up and grab it.—Don't spill nothin' on the tablecloth, or like's not Mis' Bird'll send yer away from the table—'n' I hope she will if yer do! (Susan! keep your handkerchief in your lap where Peory can borry it if she needs it, 'n' I hope she'll know when she does need it, though I don't expect it.) Now we'll try a few things ter see how they'll go! Mr. Clement, do you eat cramb'ry sarse?"

"Bet yer life!" cried Clem, who in the excitement of the moment had not taken in the idea exactly and had mistaken this for an ordinary bosom-of-the-family question.

"Clement McGrill Ruggles, do you mean to tell me that you'd say that to a dinner-party? I'll give ye one more chance. Mr. Clement, will you take some of the cramb'ry?"

"Yes, marm, thank ye kindly, if you happen ter have any handy."

"Very good, indeed! But they won't give yer two tries to-night,—yer just remember that!—Miss Peory, do you speak for white or dark meat?"

"I ain't perticler as ter color,—anything that nobody else wants will suit me," answered Peory with her best air.

"First-rate! Nobody could speak more genteel than that. Miss Kitty, will you have hard or soft sarse with your pudden?"

"Hard or soft? Oh! A little of both, if you please, an' I'm much obliged," said Kitty, bowing with decided ease and grace; at which all the other Ruggleses pointed the finger of shame at her, and Peter *grunted* expressively, that their meaning might not be mistaken.

"You just stop your gruntin', Peter Ruggles; that warn't greedy, that was all right. I wish I could git it inter your heads that it ain't so much what yer say, as the way you say it. And don't keep starin' cross-eyed at your necktie pin, or I'll take it out 'n' sew it on to Clem or Cornelius: Sarah Maud'll keep her eye on it, 'n' if it turns broken side out she'll tell yer. Gracious! I shouldn't think you'd ever seen nor worn no jool'ry in your life.—Eily, you an' Larry's too little to train, so you just look at the rest an' do's they do, 'n' the Lord have mercy on ye 'n' help ye to act decent! Now, is there anything more ye'd like to practice?"

"If yer tell me one more thing, I can't set up an' eat," said Peter gloomily; "I'm so cram full o' manners now I'm ready ter bust, 'thout no dinner at all."

"Me too," chimed in Cornelius.

"Well, I'm sorry for yer both," rejoined Mrs. Ruggles sarcastically; "if the 'mount o' manners yer've got on hand now troubles ye, you're dreadful easy hurt! Now, Sarah Maud, after dinner, about once in so often, you must git up 'n' say, 'I guess we'd better be goin';' 'n' if they say, 'Oh, no, set a while longer,' yer can set; but if they don't say nothin' you've got ter get up 'n' go.—Now hev yer got that int' yer head?"

"*About once in so often!*" Could any words in the language be fraught with more terrible and wearing uncertainty?

"Well," answered Sarah Maud mournfully, "seems as if this whole dinner-party set right square on top o' me! Mebbe I could manage my own manners, but to manage nine mannerses is worse 'n staying to home!"

"Oh, don't fret," said her mother, good-naturedly, now that the lesson was over; "I guess you'll git along. I wouldn't mind if folks would only say, 'Oh, childern will be childern;' but they won't. They'll say, 'Land o' Goodness, who fetched them childern up?'—It's quarter past five, 'n' yer can go now:—remember 'bout the hats,—don't all talk ter once,—Susan, lend yer han'k'chief ter Peory,—Peter, don't keep screwin' yer scarf-pin,—Cornelius, hold yer head up straight,—Sarah Maud, don't take yer eyes off o' Larry, 'n' Larry you keep holt o' Sarah Maud 'n' do jest as she says,—'n' whatever you do, all of yer, never forget for one second that yer mother was a McGrill."

VI

"WHEN THE PIE WAS OPENED, THE BIRDS BEGAN TO SING!"

he children went out of the back door quietly, and were presently lost to sight, Sarah Maud slipping and stumbling along absent-mindedly, as she recited rapidly under her breath, "Itwassuchapleasantevenin'n'suchashortwalk, that wethoughtwe'dleaveourhatstohome.—Itwassucha pleasantevenin'n'suchashortwalk,thatwethoughtwe'd leaveourhatstohome."

Peter rang the door-bell, and presently a servant admitted them, and, whispering something in Sarah's ear, drew her downstairs into the kitchen. The other Ruggleses stood in horror-stricken groups as the door closed behind their commanding officer; but there was no time for reflection, for a voice from above was heard, saying, "Come right up stairs, please!"

"Theirs not to make reply,Theirs not to reason why,Theirs but to do or die."

Accordingly they walked upstairs, and Elfrida, the nurse, ushered them into a room more splendid than anything they had ever seen. But, oh woe! where was Sarah Maud! and was it Fate that Mrs. Bird should say, at once, "Did you lay your hats in the hall?" Peter felt himself elected by circumstance the head of the family, and, casting one imploring look at tongue-tied Susan, standing next him, said huskily, "It was so very pleasant—that—that"——"That we hadn't good hats enough to go 'round," put in little Susan, bravely, to help him out, and then froze with horror that the ill-fated words had slipped off her tongue.

However, Mrs. Bird said, pleasantly, "Of course you wouldn't wear hats such a short distance—I forgot when I asked. Now will you come right in to Miss Carol's room? She is so anxious to see you."

Just then Sarah Maud came up the back stairs, so radiant with joy from her secret interview with the cook that Peter could have pinched her with a clear conscience; and Carol gave them a joyful welcome. "But where is Baby Larry?" she cried, looking over the group with searching eye. "Didn't he come?"

"Larry! Larry!" Good gracious, where was Larry? They were all sure that he had come in with them, for Susan remembered scolding him for tripping over the door-mat. Uncle Jack went into convulsions of laughter. "Are you sure there were nine of you?" he asked, merrily.

"I think so, sir," said Peoria, timidly; "but anyhow, there was Larry;" and she showed signs of weeping.

"Oh, well, cheer up!" cried Uncle Jack. "Probably he's not lost—only mislaid. I'll go and find him before you can say Jack Robinson!"

"I'll go, too, if you please, sir," said Sarah Maud, "for it was my place to mind him, an' if he's lost I can't relish my vittles!"

The other Ruggleses stood rooted to the floor. Was this a dinner-party, forsooth; and if so, why were such things ever spoken of as festive occasions?

Sarah Maud went out through the hall, calling, "Larry! Larry!" and without any interval of suspense a thin voice piped up from below, "Here I be!"

The truth was that Larry, being deserted by his natural guardian, dropped behind the rest, and wriggled into the hat-tree to wait for her, having no notion of walking unprotected into the jaws of a fashionable entertainment. Finding that she did not come, he tried to crawl from his refuge and call somebody, when—dark and dreadful ending to a tragic day—he found that he was too much intertwined with umbrellas and canes to move a single step. He was afraid to yell (when I have said this of Larry Ruggles I have pictured a state of helpless terror that ought to wring tears from every eye); and the sound of Sarah Maud's beloved voice, some seconds later, was like a strain of angel music in his ears. Uncle Jack dried his tears, carried him upstairs, and soon had him in breathless fits of laughter, while Carol so made the other Ruggleses forget themselves that they were presently talking like accomplished diners-out.

Carol's bed had been moved into the farthest corner of the room, and she was lying on the outside, dressed in a wonderful dressing-gown that looked like a fleecy cloud. Her golden hair fell in fluffy curls over her white forehead and neck, her cheeks flushed delicately, her eyes beamed with joy, and the children told their mother, afterwards, that she looked as beautiful as the angels in the picture books.

There was a great bustle behind a huge screen in another part of the room, and at half past five this was taken away, and the Christmas dinner-table stood revealed. What a wonderful sight it was to the poor little Ruggles children, who ate their sometimes scanty meals on the kitchen table! It blazed with tall colored candles, it gleamed with glass and silver, it blushed with flowers, it groaned with good things to eat; so it was not strange that the Ruggleses, forgetting altogether that their mother was a McGrill, shrieked in admiration of the fairy spectacle. But Larry's behavior was the most disgraceful, for he stood not upon the order of his going, but went at once for a high chair that pointed unmistakably to him, climbed up like a squirrel, gave a comprehensive look at the turkey, clapped his hands in ecstasy, rested his fat arms on the table, and cried with joy, "I beat the hull lot o' yer!" Carol laughed until she cried, giving orders, meanwhile,—"Uncle Jack, please sit at the head, Sarah Maud at the foot, and that will leave four on each side; Mamma is going to help Elfrida, so that the children need not look after each other, but just have a good time."

A sprig of holly lay by each plate, and nothing would do but each little Ruggles must leave his seat and have it pinned on by Carol, and as each course was served, one of them pleaded to take something to her. There was hurrying to and fro, I can assure you, for it is quite a difficult matter to serve a Christmas dinner on the third floor of a great city house; but if it had been necessary to carry every dish up a rope ladder the servants would gladly have done so. There were turkey and chicken, with delicious gravy and stuffing, and there were half a dozen vegetables, with cranberry jelly, and celery, and pickles; and as for the way these delicacies were served, the Ruggleses never forgot it as long as they lived.

Peter nudged Kitty, who sat next him, and said, "Look, will yer, ev'ry feller's got his own partic'lar butter; I s'pose that's to show you can eat that 'n' no more. No, it ain't either, for that pig of a Peory's just gettin' another helpin'!"

"Yes," whispered Kitty, "an' the napkins is marked with big red letters! I wonder if that's so nobody'll nip 'em; an' oh, Peter, look at the pictures stickin' right on ter the dishes! Did yee ever?"

"The plums is all took out o' my cramb'ry sarse an' it's friz to a stiff jell'!" whispered Peoria, in wild excitement.

"Hi—yah! I got a wish-bone!" sang Larry, regardless of Sarah Maud's frown; after which she asked to have his seat changed, giving as excuse that he "gen'ally set beside her, an' would feel strange;" the true reason being that she desired to kick him gently, under the table, whenever he passed what might be termed "the McGrill line."

"I declare to goodness," murmured Susan, on the other side, "there's so much to look at I can't scarcely eat nothin'!"

"Bet yer life I can!" said Peter, who had kept one servant busily employed ever since he sat down; for, luckily, no one was asked by Uncle Jack whether he would have a second helping, but the dishes were quietly passed under their noses, and not a single Ruggles refused anything that was offered him, even unto the seventh time.

Then, when Carol and Uncle Jack perceived that more turkey was a physical impossibility, the meats were taken off and the dessert was brought in—a dessert that would have frightened a strong man after such a dinner as had preceded it. Not so the Ruggleses—for a strong man is nothing to a small boy—and they kindled to the dessert as if the turkey had been a dream and the six vegetables an optical delusion. There were plum-pudding, mince-pie, and ice-cream; and there were nuts, and raisins, and oranges. Kitty chose ice-cream, explaining that she knew it "by sight, though she hadn't never tasted none;" but all the rest took the entire variety, without any regard to consequences.

"THE RUGGLESES NEVER FORGOT IT"

"My dear child," whispered Uncle Jack, as he took Carol an orange, "there is no doubt about the necessity of this feast, but I do advise you after this to have them twice a year, or quarterly perhaps, for the way these children eat is positively dangerous; I assure you I tremble for that terrible Peoria. I'm going to run races with her after dinner."

"Never mind," laughed Carol; "let them have enough for once; it does my heart good to see them, and they shall come oftener next year."

The feast being over, the Ruggleses lay back in their chairs languidly, like little gorged boa-constrictors, and the table was cleared in a trice. Then a door was opened into the next room, and there, in a corner facing Carol's bed, which had been wheeled as close as possible, stood the brilliantly lighted Christmas tree, glittering with gilded walnuts and tiny silver balloons, and wreathed with snowy chains of pop-corn. The presents had been bought mostly with Carol's story-money, and were selected after long consultations with Mrs. Bird. Each girl had a blue knitted hood, and each boy a red crocheted comforter, all made by Mamma, Carol, and Elfrida. ("Because if you buy everything, it doesn't show so much love," said Carol.) Then every girl had a pretty plaid dress of a different color, and every boy a warm coat of the right size. Here the useful presents stopped, and they were quite enough; but Carol had pleaded to give them something "for fun." "I know they need the clothes," she had said, when they were talking over the matter just after Thanksgiving, "but they don't care much for them, after all. Now, Papa, won't you *please* let me go without part of my presents this year, and give me the money they would cost, to buy something to amuse the Ruggleses?"

"You can have both," said Mr. Bird, promptly; "is there any need of my little girl's going without her own Christmas, I should like to know? Spend all the money you like."

"But that isn't the thing," objected Carol, nestling close to her father; "it wouldn't be mine. What is the use? Haven't I almost everything already, and am I not the happiest girl in the world this year, with Uncle Jack and Donald at home? You know very well it is more blessed to give than to receive; so why won't you let me do it? You never look half as happy when you are getting your presents as when you are giving us ours. Now, Papa, submit, or I shall have to be very firm and disagreeable with you!"

"Very well, your Highness, I surrender."

"That's a dear Papa! Now what were you going to give me? Confess!"

"A bronze figure of Santa Claus; and in the 'little round belly that shakes when he laughs like a bowlful of jelly,' is a wonderful clock—oh, you would never give it up if you could see it!"

"Nonsense," laughed Carol; "as I never have to get up to breakfast, nor go to bed, nor catch trains, I think my old clock will do very well! Now, Mamma, what were you going to give me?"

"Oh, I hadn't decided. A few more books, and a gold thimble, and a smelling-bottle, and a music-box, perhaps."

"Poor Carol," laughed the child, merrily, "she can afford to give up these lovely things, for there will still be left Uncle Jack, and Donald, and Paul, and Hugh, and Uncle Rob, and Aunt Elsie, and a dozen other people to fill her Christmas stocking!"

So Carol had her way, as she generally did; but it was usually a good way, which was fortunate, under the circumstances; and Sarah Maud had a set of Miss Alcott's books, and Peter a modest silver watch, Cornelius a tool-chest, Clement a dog-house for his lame puppy, Larry a magnificent Noah's ark, and each of the younger girls a beautiful doll.

You can well believe that everybody was very merry and very thankful. All the family, from Mr. Bird down to the cook, said that they had never seen so much happiness in the space of three hours; but it had to end, as all things do. The candles flickered and went out, the tree was left alone with its gilded ornaments, and Mrs. Bird sent the children downstairs at half past eight, thinking that Carol looked tired.

"Now, my darling, you have done quite enough for one day," said Mrs. Bird, getting Carol into her little nightgown. "I'm afraid you will feel worse tomorrow, and that would be a sad ending to such a charming evening."

"Oh, wasn't it a lovely, lovely time," sighed Carol. "From first to last, everything was just right. I shall never forget Larry's face when he looked at the turkey; nor Peter's when he saw his watch; nor that sweet, sweet Kitty's smile when she kissed her dolly; nor the tears in poor, dull Sarah Maud's eyes when she thanked me for her books; nor"—

"But we mustn't talk any longer about it tonight," said Mrs. Bird, anxiously; "you are too tired, dear."

"I am not so very tired, Mamma. I have felt well all day; not a bit of pain anywhere. Perhaps this has done me good."

"Perhaps; I hope so. There was no noise or confusion; it was just a merry time. Now, may I close the door and leave you alone, dear? Papa and I will steal in softly by and by to see if you are all right; but I think you need to be very quiet."

"Oh, I'm willing to stay by myself; but I am not sleepy yet, and I am going to hear the music, you know."

"Yes, I have opened the window a little, and put the screen in front of it, so that you won't feel the air."

"Can I have the shutters open? and won't you turn my bed, please? This morning I woke ever so early, and one bright, beautiful star shone in that eastern window. I never noticed it before, and I thought of the Star in the East, that guided the wise men to the place where the baby Jesus was. Good-night, Mamma. Such a happy, happy day!"

"Good-night, my precious Christmas Carol—mother's blessed Christmas child."

"Bend your head a minute, mother dear," whispered Carol, calling her mother back. "Mamma, dear, I do think that we have kept Christ's birthday this time just as He would like it. Don't you?"

"I am sure of it," said Mrs. Bird, softly.

VII

The Birdling Flies Away

he Ruggleses had finished a last romp in the library with Paul and Hugh, and Uncle Jack had taken them home and stayed a while to chat with Mrs. Ruggles, who opened the door for them, her face all aglow with excitement and delight. When Kitty and Clem showed her the oranges and nuts that they had kept for her, she astonished them by saying that at six o'clock Mrs. Bird had sent her in the finest dinner she had ever seen in her life; and not only that, but a piece of dress-goods that must have cost a dollar a yard if it cost a cent.

As Uncle Jack went down the rickety steps he looked back into the window for a last glimpse of the family, as the children gathered about their mother, showing their beautiful presents again and again,—and then upward to a window in the great house yonder. "A little child shall lead them," he thought. "Well, if—if anything ever happens to Carol, I will take the Ruggleses under my wing."

"Softly, Uncle Jack," whispered the boys, as he walked into the library a while later. "We are listening to the music in the church. The choir has sung 'Carol, brothers, carol,' and now we think the organist is beginning to play 'My ain countree' for Carol."

"I hope she hears it," said Mrs. Bird; "but they are very late to-night, and I dare not speak to her lest she should be asleep. It is almost ten o'clock."

"I am far frae my hame,I am weary aften whilesFor the langed-for hame-bringin',An' my Faether's welcome smilesAn' I'll ne'er be fu' content,Until my e'en do seeThe gowden gates o' heavenIn my ain countree.

"MY AIN COUNTREE"

"The earth is decked wi' flow'rs,Mony tinted, fresh an' gay,An' the birdies warble blythely,For my Faether made them sae;But these sights an' these soun'sWill as naething be to me,When I hear the angels singin'In my ain countree.

"Like a bairn to its mither,A wee birdie to its nest,I fain would be gangin' nooUnto my Faether's breast;For He gathers in His armsHelpless, worthless lambs like me,An' carries them Himsel'To his ain countree."

There were tears in many eyes, but not in Carol's. The loving heart had quietly ceased to beat, and the "wee birdie" in the great house had flown to its "home nest." Carol had fallen asleep! But as to the song, I think perhaps, I cannot say, she heard it after all!

So sad an ending to a happy day! Perhaps—to those who were left; and yet Carol's mother, even in the freshness of her grief, was glad that her darling had slipped away on the loveliest day of her life, out of its glad content, into everlasting peace.

She was glad that she had gone as she had come, on the wings of song, when all the world was brimming over with joy; glad of every grateful smile, of every joyous burst of laughter, of every loving thought and word and deed the dear last day had brought.

Sadness reigned, it is true, in the little house behind the garden; and one day poor Sarah Maud, with a courage born of despair, threw on her hood and shawl, walked straight to a certain house a mile away, up the marble steps into good Dr. Bartol's office, falling at his feet as she cried, "Oh, sir, it was me an' our children that went to Miss Carol's last dinner-party, an' if we made her worse we can't never be happy again!" Then the kind old gentleman took her rough hand in his and told her to dry her tears, for neither she nor any of her flock had hastened Carol's flight; indeed, he said that had it not been for the strong hopes and wishes that filled her tired heart, she could not have stayed long enough to keep that last merry Christmas with her dear ones.

And so the old years, fraught with memories, die, one after another, and the new years, bright with hopes, are born to take their places; but Carol lives again in every chime of Christmas bells that peal glad tidings, and in every Christmas anthem sung by childish voices.

End

THE OLD PEABODY PEW

A Christmas Romance of a Country Church

BY

KATE DOUGLAS WIGGIN

The Old Peabody Pew

CHAPTER I

Edgewood, like all the other villages along the banks of the Saco, is full of sunny slopes and leafy hollows. There are little, rounded, green-clad hillocks that might, like their scriptural sisters, "skip with joy," and there are grand, rocky hills tufted with gaunt pine trees—these leading the eye to the splendid heights of a neighbour State, where snow-crowned peaks tower in the blue distance, sweeping the horizon in a long line of majesty.

Tory Hill holds its own among the others for peaceful beauty and fair prospect, and on its broad, level summit sits the white-painted Orthodox Meeting-House. This faces a grassy common where six roads meet, as if the early settlers had determined that no one should lack salvation because of a difficulty in reaching its visible source.

The old church has had a dignified and fruitful past, dating from that day in 1761 when young Paul Coffin received his call to preach at a stipend of fifty pounds sterling a year; answering "that never having heard of any Uneasiness among the people about his Doctrine or manner of life, he declared himself pleased to Settle as Soon as might be Judged Convenient."

But that was a hundred and fifty years ago, and much has happened since those simple, strenuous old days. The chastening hand of time has been laid somewhat heavily on the town as well as on the church. Some of her sons have marched to the wars and died on the field of honour; some, seeking better fortunes, have gone westward; others, wearying of village life, the rocky soil, and rigours of farm-work, have become entangled in the noise and competition, the rush and strife, of cities. When the sexton rings the bell nowadays, on a Sunday morning, it seems to have lost some of its old-time militant strength, something of its hope and courage; but it still rings, and although the Davids and Solomons, the Matthews, Marks, and Pauls of former congregations have left few descendants to perpetuate their labours, it will go on ringing as long as there is a Tabitha, a Dorcas, a Lois, or a Eunice left in the community.

This sentiment had been maintained for a quarter of a century, but it was now especially strong, as the old Tory Hill Meeting-House had been undergoing for several years more or less extensive repairs. In point of fact, the still stronger word, "improvements," might be used with impunity; though whenever the Dorcas Society, being female, and therefore possessed of notions regarding comfort and beauty, suggested any serious changes, the finance committees, which were inevitably male in their composition, generally disapproved of making any impious alterations in a tabernacle, chapel, temple, or any other building used for purposes of worship. The majority in these august bodies asserted that their ancestors had prayed and sung there for a century and a quarter, and what was good enough for their ancestors was entirely suitable for them. Besides, the community was becoming less and less prosperous, and church-going was growing more and more lamentably uncommon, so that even from a business standpoint, any sums expended upon decoration by a poor and struggling parish would be worse than wasted.

In the particular year under discussion in this story, the valiant and progressive Mrs. Jeremiah Burbank was the president of the Dorcas Society, and she remarked privately and publicly that if her ancestors liked a smoky church, they had a perfect right to the enjoyment of it, but that she didn't intend to sit through meeting on winter Sundays, with her white ostrich feather turning grey and her eyes smarting and watering, for the rest of her natural life.

Whereupon, this being in a business session, she then and there proposed to her already hypnotized constituents ways of earning enough money to build a new chimney on the other side of the church.

An awe-stricken community witnessed this beneficent act of vandalism, and, finding that no thunderbolts of retribution descended from the skies, greatly relished the change. If one or two aged persons complained that they could not sleep as sweetly during sermon-time in the now clear atmosphere of the church, and that the parson's eye was keener than before, why, that was a mere detail, and could not be avoided; what was the loss of a little sleep compared with the discoloration of Mrs. Jere Burbank's white ostrich feather and the smarting of Mrs. Jere Burbank's eyes?

A new furnace followed the new chimney, in due course, and as a sense of comfort grew, there was opportunity to notice the lack of beauty. Twice in sixty years had some well-to-do summer parishioner painted the interior of the church at his own expense; but although the roof had been many times reshingled, it had always persisted in leaking, so that the ceiling and walls were disfigured by unsightly spots and stains and streaks. The question of shingling was tacitly felt to be outside the feminine domain, but as there were five women to one man in the church membership, the feminine domain was frequently obliged to extend its limits into the hitherto unknown. Matters of tarring and water-proofing were discussed in and out of season, and the very school-children imbibed knowledge concerning lapping, overlapping, and cross-lapping, and first and second quality of cedar shingles. Miss Lobelia Brewster, who had a rooted distrust of anything done by mere man, created strife by remarking that she could have stopped the leak in the belfry tower with her red flannel petticoat better than the Milltown man with his new-fangled rubber sheeting, and that the last shingling could have been more thoroughly done by a "female infant babe"; whereupon the person criticized retorted that he wished Miss Lobelia Brewster had a few infant babes to "put on the job—he'd like to see 'em try." Meantime several male members of the congregation, who at one time or another had sat on the roof during the hottest of the dog days to see that shingling operations we're conscientiously and skilfully performed, were very pessimistic as to any satisfactory result ever being achieved.

"The angle of the roof—what they call the 'pitch'—they say that that's always been wrong," announced the secretary of the Dorcas in a business session.

"Is it that kind of pitch that the Bible says you can't touch without being defiled? If not, I vote that we unshingle the roof and alter the pitch!" This proposal came from a sister named Maria Sharp, who had valiantly offered the year before to move the smoky chimney with her own hands, if the "men-folks" wouldn't.

But though the incendiary suggestion of altering the pitch was received with applause at the moment, subsequent study of the situation proved that such a proceeding was entirely beyond the modest means of the society. Then there arose an ingenious and militant carpenter in a neighbouring village, who asserted that he would shingle the meeting-house roof for such and such a sum, and agree to drink every drop of water that would leak in afterward. This was felt by all parties to be a promise attended by extraordinary risks, but it was accepted nevertheless, Miss Lobelia Brewster remarking that the rash carpenter, being already married, could not marry a Dorcas anyway, and even if he died, he was not a resident of Edgewood, and therefore could be more easily spared, and that it would be rather exciting, just for a change, to see a man drink himself to death with rain-water. The expected tragedy never occurred, however, and the inspired shingler fulfilled his promise to the letter, so that before many months the Dorcas Society proceeded, with incredible exertion, to earn more money, and the interior of the church was neatly painted and made as fresh as a rose. With no smoke, no rain, no snow nor melting ice to defile it, the good old landmark that had been pointing its finger Heavenward for over a century would now be clean and fragrant for years to come, and the weary sisters leaned back in their respective rocking-chairs and drew deep breaths of satisfaction.

These breaths continued to be drawn throughout an unusually arduous haying season; until, in fact, a visitor from a neighbouring city was heard to remark that the Tory Hill Meeting-House would be one of the best preserved and pleasantest churches in the whole State of Maine, if only it were suitably carpeted.

This thought had secretly occurred to many a Dorcas in her hours of pie-making, preserving, or cradle-rocking, but had been promptly extinguished as flagrantly extravagant and altogether impossible. Now that it had been openly mentioned, the contagion of the idea spread, and in a month every sort of honest machinery for the increase of funds had been set in motion: harvest suppers, pie sociables, old folk's concerts, apron sales, and, as a last resort, a subscription paper, for the church floor measured hundreds of square yards, and the carpet committee announce that a good ingrain could not be purchased, even with the church discount, for less than ninety-seven cents a yard.

The Dorcases took out their pencils, and when they multiplied the surface of the floor by the price of the carpet per yard, each Dorcas attaining a result entirely different from all the others, there was a shriek of dismay, especially from the secretary, who had included in her mathematical operation certain figures in her possession representing the cubical contents of the church and the offending pitch of the roof, thereby obtaining a product that would have dismayed a Croesus. Time sped and efforts increased, but the Dorcases were at length obliged to clip the wings of their desire and content themselves with carpeting the pulpit and pulpit steps, the choir, and the two aisles, leaving the floor in the pews until some future year.

How the women cut and contrived and matched that hardly-bought red ingrain carpet, in the short December afternoons that ensued after its purchase; so that, having failed to be ready for Thanksgiving, it could be finished for the Christmas festivities!

They were sewing in the church, and as the last stitches were being taken, Maria Sharp suddenly ejaculated in her impulsive fashion:—

"Wouldn't it have been just perfect if we could have had the pews repainted before we laid the new carpet!"

"It would, indeed," the president answered; "but it will take us all winter to pay for the present improvements, without any thought of fresh paint. If only we had a few more men-folks to help along!"

"Or else none at all!" was Lobelia Brewster's suggestion. "It's havin' so few that keeps us all stirred up. If there wa'n't any anywheres, we'd have women deacons and carpenters and painters, and get along first rate; for somehow the supply o' women always holds out, same as it does with caterpillars an' flies an' grasshoppers!"

Everybody laughed, although Maria Sharp asserted that she for one was not willing to be called a caterpillar simply because there were too many women in the universe.

"I never noticed before how shabby and scarred and dirty the pews are," said the minister's wife as she looked at them reflectively.

"I've been thinking all the afternoon of the story about the poor old woman and the lily," and Nancy Wentworth's clear voice broke into the discussion. "Do you remember some one gave her a stalk of Easter lilies and she set them in a glass pitcher on the kitchen table? After looking at them for a few minutes, she got up from her chair and washed the pitcher until the glass shone. Sitting down again, she glanced at the little window. It would never do; she had forgotten how dusty and blurred it was, and she took her cloth and burnished the panes. Then she scoured the table, then the floor, then blackened the stove before she sat down to her knitting. And of course the lily had done it all, just by showing, in its whiteness, how grimy everything else was."

The minister's wife who had been in Edgewood only a few months, looked admiringly at Nancy's bright face, wondering that five-and-thirty years of life, including ten of school-teaching, had done so little to mar its serenity. "The lily story is as true as the gospel!" she exclaimed, "and I can see how one thing has led you to another in making the church comfortable. But my husband says that two coats of paint on the pews would cost a considerable sum."

"How about cleaning them? I don't believe they've had a good hard washing since the flood." The suggestion came from Deacon Miller's wife to the president.

"They can't even be scrubbed for less than fifteen or twenty dollars, for I thought of that and asked Mrs. Simpson yesterday, and she said twenty cents a pew was the cheapest she could do it for."

"We've done everything else," said Nancy Wentworth, with a twitch of her thread; "why don't we scrub the pews? There's nothing in the orthodox creed to forbid, is there?"

"Speakin' o' creeds," and here old Mrs. Sargent paused in her work, "Elder Ransom from Acreville stopped with us last night, an' he tells me they recite the Euthanasian Creed every few Sundays in the Episcopal Church. I didn't want him to know how ignorant I was, but I looked up the word in the dictionary. It means easy death, and I can't see any sense in that, though it's a terrible long creed, the Elder says, an' if it's any longer 'n ourn, I should think anybody might easy die learnin' it!"

"I think the word is Athanasian," ventured the minister's wife.

"Elder Ransom's always plumb full o' doctrine," asserted Miss Brewster, pursuing the subject. "For my part, I'm glad he preferred Acreville to our place. He was so busy bein' a minister, he never got round to bein' a human creeter. When he used to comc to sociables and picnics, always lookin' kind o' like the potato blight, I used to think how complete he'd be if he had a foldin' pulpit under his coat tails; they make foldin' beds nowadays, an' I s'pose they could make foldin' pulpits, if there was a call."

"Land sakes, I hope there won't be!" exclaimed Mrs. Sargent. "An' the Elder never said much of anything either, though he was always preachin'! Now your husband, Mis' Baxter, always has plenty to say after you think he's all through. There's water in his well when the others is all dry!"

"But how about the pews?" interrupted Mrs. Burbank. "I think Nancy's idea is splendid, and I want to see it carried out. We might make it a picnic, bring our luncheons, and work all together; let every woman in the congregation come and scrub her own pew."

"Some are too old, others live at too great a distance," and the minister's wife sighed a little; "indeed, most of those who once owned the pews or sat in them seemed to be dead, or gone away to live in busier places."

"I've no patience with 'em, gallivantin' over the earth," and here Lobelia rose and shook the carpet threads from her lap. "I shouldn't want to live in a livelier place than Edgewood, seem's though! We wash and hang out Mondays, iron Tuesdays, cook Wednesdays, clean house and mend Thursdays and Fridays, bake Saturdays, and go to meetin' Sundays. I don't hardly see how they can do any more 'n that in Chicago!"

"Never mind if we have lost members!" said the indomitable Mrs. Burbank. "The members we still have left must work all the harder. We'll each clean our own pew, then take a few of our neighbours', and then hire Mrs. Simpson to do the wainscoting and floor. Can we scrub Friday and lay the carpet Saturday? My husband and Deacon Miller can help us at the end of the week. All in favour manifest it by the usual sign. Contrary minded? It is a vote."

There never were any contrary minded when Mrs. Jere Burbank was in the chair. Public sentiment in Edgewood was swayed by the Dorcas Society, but Mrs. Burbank swayed the Dorcases themselves as the wind sways the wheat.

CHAPTER II

The old Meeting House wore an animated aspect when the eventful Friday came, a cold, brilliant, sparkling December day, with good sleighing, and with energy in every breath that swept over the dazzling snowfields. The sexton had built a fire in the furnace on the way to his morning work—a fire so economically contrived that it would last exactly the four or five necessary hours, and not a second more. At eleven o'clock all the pillars of the society had assembled, having finished their own household work and laid out on their respective kitchen tables comfortable luncheons for the men of the family, if they were fortunate enough to number any among their luxuries. Water was heated upon oil-stoves set about here and there, and there was a brave array of scrubbing-brushes, cloths, soap, and even sand and soda, for it had been decided and manifested-by-the-usual-sign-and-no-contrary-minded-and-it-was-a-vote that the dirt was to come off, whether the paint came with it or not. Each of the fifteen women present selected a block of seats, preferably one in which her own was situated, and all fell busily to work.

"There is nobody here to clean the right-wing pews," said Nancy Wentworth, "so I will take those for my share."

"You're not making a very wise choice, Nancy," and the minister's wife smiled as she spoke. "The infant class of the Sunday-school sits there, you know, and I expect the paint has had extra wear and tear. Families don't seem to occupy those pews regularly nowadays."

"I can remember when every seat in the whole church was filled, wings an' all," mused Mrs. Sargent, wringing out her wascloth in a reminiscent mood. "The one in front o' you, Nancy, was always called the 'deef pew' in the old times, and all the folks that was hard o' hearin' used to congregate there."

"The next pew hasn't been occupied since I came here," said the minister's wife.

"No," answered Mrs. Sargent, glad of any opportunity to retail neighbourhood news. "'Squire Bean's folks have moved to Portland to be with the married daughter. Somebody has to stay with her, and her husband won't. The 'Squire ain't a strong man, and he's most too old to go to meetin' now. The youngest son has just died in New York, so I hear."

"What ailed him?" inquired Maria Sharp.

"I guess he was completely wore out takin' care of his health," returned Mrs. Sargent. "He had a splendid constitution from a boy, but he was always afraid it wouldn't last him.—The seat back o' 'Squire Bean's is the old Peabody pew—ain't that the Peabody pew you're scrubbin', Nancy?"

"I believe so," Nancy answered, never pausing in her labours. "It's so long since anybody sat there, it's hard to remember."

"It is the Peabodys', I know it, because the aisle runs right up facin' it. I can see old Deacon Peabody settin' in this end same as if 'twas yesterday."

"He had died before Jere and I came back here to live," said Mrs. Burbank. "The first I remember, Justin Peabody sat in the end seat; the sister that died, next, and in the corner, against the wall, Mrs. Peabody, with a crêpe shawl and a palm-leaf fan. They were a handsome family. You used to sit with them sometimes, Nancy; Esther was great friends with you."

"Yes, she was," Nancy replied, lifting the tattered cushion from its place and brushing it; "and I with her.—What is the use of scrubbing and carpeting, when there are only twenty pew-cushions and six hassocks in the whole church, and most of them ragged? How can I ever mend this?"

"I shouldn't trouble myself to darn other people's cushions!"

This unchristian sentiment came in Mrs. Miller's ringing tones from the rear of the church.

"I don't know why," argued Maria Sharp. "I'm going to mend my Aunt Achsa's cushion, and we haven't spoken for years; but hers is the next pew to mine, and I'm going to have my part of the church look decent, even if she is too stingy to do her share. Besides, there aren't any Peabodys left to do their own darning, and Nancy was friends with Esther."

"Yes, it's nothing more than right," Nancy replied, with a note of relief in her voice, "considering Esther."

"Though he don't belong to the scrubbin' sex, there is one Peabody alive, as you know, if you stop to think, Maria; for Justin's alive, and livin' out West somewheres. At least, he's as much alive as ever he was; he was as good as dead when he was twenty-one, but his mother was always too soft-hearted to bury him."

There was considerable laughter over this sally of the outspoken Mrs. Sargent, whose keen wit was the delight of the neighbourhood.

"I know he's alive and doing business in Detroit, for I got his address a week or ten days ago, and wrote, asking him if he'd like to give a couple of dollars toward repairing the old church."

Everybody looked at Mrs. Burbank with interest.

"Hasn't he answered?" asked Maria Sharp.

Nancy Wentworth held her breath, turned her face to the wall, and silently wiped the paint of the wainscoting. The blood that had rushed into her cheeks at Mrs. Sargent's jeering reference to Justin Peabody still lingered there for any one who ran to read, but fortunately nobody ran; they were too busy scrubbing.

"Not yet. Folks don't hurry about answering when you ask them for a contribution," replied the president, with a cynicism common to persons who collect funds for charitable purposes. "George Wickham sent me twenty-five cents from Denver. When I wrote him a receipt, I said thank you same as Aunt Polly did when the neighbours brought her a piece of beef: 'Ever so much obleeged, but don't forget me when you come to kill a pig.'—Now, Mrs. Baxter, you shan't clean James Bruce's pew, or what was his before he turned Second Advent. I'll do that myself, for he used to be in my Sunday-school class."

"He's the backbone o' that congregation now," asserted Mrs. Sargent, "and they say he's goin' to marry Mrs. Sam Peters, who sings in their choir as soon as his year is up. They make a perfect fool of him in that church."

"You can't make a fool of a man that nature ain't begun with," argued Miss Brewster. "Jim Bruce never was very strong-minded, but I declare it seems to me that when men lose their wives, they lose their wits! I was sure Jim would marry Hannah Thompson that keeps house for him. I suspected she was lookin' out for a life job when she hired out with him."

“Hannah Thompson may keep Jim’s house, but she’ll never keep Jim, that’s certain!” affirmed the president; “and I can’t see that Mrs. Peters will better herself much.”

“I don’t blame her, for one!” came in no uncertain tones from the left-wing pews, and the Widow Buzzell rose from her knees and approached the group by the pulpit. “If there’s anything duller than cookin’ three meals a day for yourself, and settin’ down and eatin’ ’em by yourself, and then gettin’ up and clearin’ ’em away after yourself, I’d like to know it! I shouldn’t want any good-lookin’, pleasant-spoken man to offer himself to me without he expected to be snapped up, that’s all! But if you’ve made out to get one husband in York County, you can thank the Lord and not expect any more favours. I used to think Tom was poor comp’ny and complain I couldn’t have any conversation with him, but land, I could talk at him, and there’s considerable comfort in that. And I could pick up after him! Now every room in my house is clean, and every closet and bureau drawer, too; I can’t start drawin’ in another rug, for I’ve got all the rugs I can step foot on. I dried so many apples last year I shan’t need to cut up any this season. My jelly and preserves ain’t out, and there I am; and there most of us are, in this village, without a man to take steps for and trot ’round after! There’s just three husbands among the fifteen women scrubbin’ here now, and the rest of us is all old maids and widders. No wonder the men-folks die, or move away like Justin Peabody; a place with such a mess o’ women-folks ain’t healthy to live in, whatever Lobelia Brewster may say.”

CHAPTER III

Justin Peabody had once faithfully struggled with the practical difficulties of life in Edgewood, or so he had thought, in those old days of which Nancy Wentworth was thinking as she wiped the paint of the Peabody pew. Work in the mills did not attract him; he had no capital to invest in a stock of goods for store-keeping; school-teaching offered him only a pittance; there remained then only the farm, if he were to stay at home and keep his mother company.

"Justin don't seem to take no holt of things," said the neighbours.

"Good Heavens!" It seemed to him that there were no things to take hold of! That was his first thought; later he grew to think that the trouble all lay in himself, and both thoughts bred weakness.

The farm had somehow supported the family in the old Deacon's time, but Justin seemed unable to coax a competence from the soil. He could, and did, rise early and work late; till the earth, sow crops; but he could not make the rain fall nor the sun shine at the times he needed them, and the elements, however much they might seem to favour his neighbours, seldom smiled on his enterprises. The crows liked Justin's corn better than any other in Edgewood. It had a richness peculiar to itself, a quality that appealed to the most jaded palate, so that it was really worth while to fly over a mile of intervening fields and pay it the delicate compliment of preference.

Justin could explain the attitude of caterpillars, worms, grasshoppers, and potato-bugs toward him only by assuming that he attracted them as the magnet in the toy boxes attracts the miniature fishes.

"Land of liberty! look at 'em congregate!" ejaculated Jabe Slocum, when he was called in for consultation. "Now if you'd gone in for breedin' insecks, you could be as proud as Cuffy an' exhibit 'em at the County Fair! They'd give yer prizes for size an' numbers an' speed, I guess! Why, say, they're real crowded for room—the plants ain't give 'em enough leaves to roost on! Have you tried 'Bug Death'?"

"It acts like a tonic on them," said Justin gloomily.

"Sho! you don't say so! Now mine can't abide the sight nor smell of it. What 'bout Paris green?"

"They thrive on it; it's as good as an appetizer."

"Well," said Jabe Slocum, revolving the quid of tobacco in his mouth reflectively, "the bug that ain't got no objection to p'ison is a bug that's got ways o' thinkin' an' feelin' an' reasonin' that I ain't able to cope with! P'r'aps it's all a leadin' o' Providence. Mebbe it shows you'd ought to quit farmin' crops an' take to raisin' live stock!"

Justin did just that, as a matter of fact, a year or two later; but stock that has within itself the power of being "live" has also rare qualifications for being dead when occasion suits, and it generally did suit Justin's stock. It proved prone not only to all the general diseases that cattle-flesh is heir to, but was capable even of suicide. At least, it is true that two valuable Jersey calves, tied to stakes on the hillside, had flung themselves violently down the bank and strangled themselves with their own ropes in a manner which seemed to show that they found no pleasure in existence, at all events on the Peabody farm.

These were some of the little tragedies that had sickened young Justin Peabody with life in Edgewood, and Nancy Wentworth, even then, realized some of them and sympathized without speaking, in a girl's poor, helpless way.

Mrs. Simpson had washed the floor in the right wing of the church and Nancy had cleaned all the paint. Now she sat in the old Peabody pew darning the forlorn, faded cushion with grey carpet-thread: thread as grey as her own life.

The scrubbing-party had moved to its labours in a far corner of the church, and two of the women were beginning preparations for the basket luncheons. Nancy's needle was no busier than her memory. Long years ago she had often sat in the Peabody pew, sometimes at first as a girl of sixteen when asked by Esther, and then, on coming home from school at eighteen, "finished," she had been invited now and again by Mrs. Peabody herself, on those Sundays when her own invalid mother had not attended service.

Those were wonderful Sundays—Sundays of quiet, trembling peace and maiden joy.

Justin sat beside her, and she had been sure then, but had long since grown to doubt the evidence of her senses, that he, too, vibrated with pleasure at the nearness. Was there not a summer morning when his hand touched her white lace mitt as they held the hymn-book together, and the lines of the

Rise, my soul, and stretch thy wings,
Thy better portion trace,

became blurred on the page and melted into something indistinguishable for a full minute or two afterward? Were there not looks, and looks, and looks? Or had she some misleading trick of vision in those days? Justin's dark, handsome profile rose before her: the level brows and fine lashes; the well-cut nose and lovable mouth—the Peabody mouth and chin, somewhat too sweet and pliant for strength, perhaps. Then the eyes turned to hers in the old way, just for a fleeting glance, as they had so often done at prayer-meeting, or sociable, or Sunday service. Was it not a man's heart she had seen in them? And oh, if she could only be sure that her own woman's heart had not looked out from hers, drawn from its maiden shelter in spite of all her wish to keep it hidden!

Then followed two dreary years of indecision and suspense, when Justin's eyes met hers less freely; when his looks were always gloomy and anxious; when affairs at the Peabody farm grew worse and worse; when his mother followed her husband, the old Deacon, and her daughter Esther to the burying-ground in the churchyard. Then the end of all things came, the end of the world for Nancy: Justin's departure for the West in a very frenzy of discouragement over the narrowness and limitation and injustice of his lot; over the rockiness and barrenness and unkindness of the New England soil; over the general bitterness of fate and the "bludgeonings of chance."

Hc was a failure, born of a family of failures. If the world owed him a living, he had yet to find the method by which it could be earned. All this he thought and uttered, and much more of the same sort. In these days of humbled pride self was paramount, though it was a self he despised. There was no time for love. Who was he for a girl to lean upon?—he who could not stand erect himself!

He bade a stiff good-bye to his neighbours, and to Nancy he vouchsafed little more. A handshake, with no thrill of love in it such as might have furnished her palm, at least, some memories to dwell upon; a few stilted words of leave-taking; a halting, meaningless sentence or two about his "botch" of life—then he walked away from the Wentworth doorstep. But half way down the garden path, where the shrivelled hollyhocks stood like sentinels, did a wave of something different sweep over him—a wave of the boyish, irresponsible past when his heart had wings and could fly without fear to its mate—a wave of the past that was rushing through Nancy's mind, well-nigh burying her in its bitter-sweet waters! For he lifted his head, and suddenly retracing his steps, he came toward her, and, taking her hand again, said forlornly: "You'll see me back when my luck turns, Nancy."

Nancy knew that the words might mean little or much, according to the manner in which they were uttered, but to her hurt pride and sore, shamed woman-instinct, they were a promise, simply because there was a choking sound in Justin's voice and tears in Justin's eyes. "You'll see me back when my luck turns, Nancy;" this was the phrase upon which she had lived for more than ten years. Nancy had once heard the old parson say, ages ago, that the whole purpose of life was the growth of the soul; that we eat, sleep, clothe ourselves, work, love, all to give the soul another day, month, year, in which to develop. She used to wonder if her soul could be growing in the monotonous round of her dull duties and her duller pleasures. She did not confess it even to herself; nevertheless she knew that she worked, ate, slept, to live until Justin's luck turned. Her love had lain in her heart a bird without a song, year after year. Her mother had dwelt by her side and never guessed; her father too; and both were dead. The neighbours also, lynx-eyed and curious, had never suspected. If she had suffered, no one in Edgewood was any the wiser, for the maiden heart is not commonly worn on the sleeve in New England. If she had been openly pledged to Justin Peabody, she could have waited twice ten years with a decent show of self-respect, for long engagements were viewed rather as a matter of course in that neighbourhood. The endless months had gone on since that grey November day when Justin had said good-bye. It had been just before Thanksgiving, and she went to church with an aching and ungrateful heart. The parson read from the eighth chapter of St. Matthew, a most unexpected selection for that holiday. "If you can't find anything else to be thankful for," he cried, "go home and be thankful you are not a leper!"

Nancy took the drastic counsel away from the church with her, and it was many a year before she could manage to add to this slender store anything to increase her gratitude for mercies given, though all the time she was outwardly busy, cheerful, and helpful.

Justin had once come back to Edgewood, and it was the bitterest drop in her cup of bitterness that she was spending that winter in Berwick (where, so the neighbours told him, she was a great favourite in society, and was receiving much attention from gentlemen), so that she had never heard of his visit until the spring had come again. Parted friends did not keep up with one another's affairs by means of epistolary communication, in those days, in Edgewood; it was not the custom. Spoken words were difficult enough to Justin Peabody, and written words were quite impossible, especially if they were to be used to define his half-conscious desires and his fluctuations of will, or to recount his disappointments and discouragements and mistakes.

CHAPTER IV

It was Saturday afternoon, the twenty-fourth of December, and the weary sisters of the Dorcas band rose from their bruised knees and removed their little stores of carpet-tacks from their mouths. This was a feminine custom of long standing, and as no village dressmaker had ever died of pins in the digestive organs, so were no symptoms of carpet-tacks ever discovered in any Dorcas, living or dead. Men wondered at the habit and reviled it, but stood confounded in the presence of its indubitable harmlessness.

The red ingrain carpet was indeed very warm, beautiful, and comforting to the eye, and the sisters were suitably grateful to Providence, and devoutly thankful to themselves, that they had been enabled to buy, sew, and lay so many yards of it. But as they stood looking at their completed task, it was cruelly true that there was much left to do.

The aisles had been painted dark brown on each side of the red strips leading from the doors to the pulpit, but the rest of the church floor was "a thing of shreds and patches." Each member of the carpet committee had paid (as a matter of pride, however ill she could afford it) three dollars and sixty-seven cents for sufficient carpet to lay in her own pew; but these brilliant spots of conscientious effort only made the stretches of bare, unpainted floor more evident. And that was not all. Traces of former spasmodic and individual efforts desecrated the present ideals. The doctor's pew had a pink and blue Brussels on it; the lawyer's, striped stair-carpeting; the Browns from Deerwander sported straw matting and were not abashed; while the Greens, the Whites, the Blacks and the Greys displayed floor coverings as dissimilar as their names.

"I never noticed it before!" exclaimed Maria Sharp, "but it ain't Christian, that floor! it's heathenish and ungodly!"

"For mercy's sake, don't swear, Maria," said Mrs. Miller nervously. "We've done our best, and let's hope that folks will look up and not down. It isn't as if they were going to set in the chandelier; they'll have something else to think about when Nancy gets her hemlock branches and white carnations in the pulpit vases. This morning my Abner picked off two pinks from the plant I've been nursing in my dining-room for weeks, trying to make it bloom for Christmas. I slapped his hands good, and it's been haunting me ever since to think I had to correct him the day before Christmas—Come, Lobelia, we must be hurrying!"

“One thing comforts me,” exclaimed the Widow Buzzell, as she took her hammer and tacks preparatory to leaving; “and that is that the Methodist meetin’-house ain’t got any carpet at all.”

“Mrs. Buzzell, Mrs. Buzzell!” interrupted the minister’s wife, with a smile that took the sting from her speech. “It will be like punishing little Abner Miller; if we think those thoughts on Christmas Eve, we shall surely be haunted afterward.”

“And anyway,” interjected Maria Sharp, who always saved the situation, “you just wait and see if the Methodists don’t say they’d rather have no carpet at all than have one that don’t go all over the floor. I know ’em!” and she put on her hood and blanket-shawl as she gave one last fond look at the improvements.

“I’m going home to get my supper, and come back afterward to lay the carpet in my pew; my beans and brown bread will be just right by now, and perhaps it will rest me a little; besides, I must feed ’Zekiel.”

As Nancy Wentworth spoke, she sat in a corner of her own modest rear seat, looking a little pale and tired. Her waving dark hair had loosened and fallen over her cheeks, and her eyes gleamed from under it wistfully. Nowadays Nancy’s eyes never had the sparkle of gazing into the future, but always the liquid softness that comes from looking backward.

“The church will be real cold by then, Nancy,” objected Mrs. Burbank.—“Good-night, Mrs. Baxter.”

“Oh, no! I shall be back by half-past six, and I shall not work long. Do you know what I believe I’ll do, Mrs. Burbank, just through the holidays? Christmas and New Year’s both coming on Sunday this year, there’ll be a great many out to church, not counting the strangers that’ll come to the special service to-morrow. Instead of putting down my own pew carpet that’ll never be noticed here in the back, I’ll lay it in the old Peabody pew, for the red aisle-strip leads straight up to it; the ministers always go up that side, and it does look forlorn.”

“That’s so! And all the more because my pew, that’s exactly opposite in the left wing, is new carpeted and cushioned,” replied the president. “I think it’s real generous of you, Nancy, because the Riverboro folks, knowing that you’re a member of the carpet committee, will be sure to notice, and think it's queer you haven't made an effort to carpet your own pew."

"Never mind!" smiled Nancy wearily. "Riverboro folks never go to bed on Saturday nights without wondering what Edgewood is thinking about them!"

The minister's wife stood at her window watching Nancy as she passed the parsonage.

"How wasted! How wasted!" she sighed. "Going home to eat her lonely supper and feed 'Zekiel . . . I can bear it for the others, but not for Nancy . . . Now she has lighted her lamp, now she has put fresh pine on the fire, for new smoke comes from the chimney. Why should I sit down and serve my dear husband, and Nancy feed 'Zekiel?"

There was some truth in Mrs. Baxter's feeling. Mrs. Buzzell, for instance, had three sons; Maria Sharp was absorbed in her lame father and her Sunday-school work; and Lobelia Brewster would not have considered matrimony a blessing, even under the most favourable conditions. But Nancy was framed and planned for other things, and 'Zekiel was an insufficient channel for her soft, womanly sympathy and her bright activity of mind and body.

'Zekiel had lost his tail in a mowing-machine; 'Zekiel had the asthma, and the immersion of his nose in milk made him sneeze, so he was wont to slip his paw in and out of the dish and lick it patiently for five minutes together. Nancy often watched him pityingly, giving him kind and gentle words to sustain his fainting spirit, but to-night she paid no heed to him, although he sneezed violently to attract her attention.

She had put her supper on the lighted table by the kitchen window and was pouring out her cup of tea, when a boy rapped at the door. "Here's a paper and a letter, Miss Wentworth," he said. "It's the second this week, and they think over to the store that that Berwick widower must be settin' up and takin' notice!"

She had indeed received a letter the day before, an unsigned communication, consisting only of the words, "Second Epistle of John. Verse 12."

She had taken her Bible to look out the reference and found it to be:—

"Having many things to write unto you, I would not write with paper and ink; but I trust to come unto you, and speak face to face, that our joy may be full."

The envelope was postmarked New York, and she smiled, thinking that Mrs. Emerson, a charming lady who had spent the summer in Edgewood, and had sung with her in the village choir, was coming back, as she had promised, to have a sleigh ride and see Edgewood in its winter dress. Nancy had almost forgotten the first letter in the excitements of her busy day, and now here was another, from Boston this time. She opened the envelope and found again only a single sentence, printed, not written. (Lest she should guess the hand, she wondered?)

"Second Epistle of John. Verse 5."

"And now I beseech thee, lady, not as though I wrote a new commandment unto thee, but that which we had from the beginning, that we love one another."

Was it Mrs. Emerson? Could it be—any one else? Was it—? No, it might have been, years ago; but not now; not now!—And yet; he was always so different from other people; and once, in church, he had handed her the hymn-book with his finger pointing to a certain verse.

She always fancied that her secret fidelity of heart rose from the fact that Justin Peabody was "different." From the hour of their first acquaintance, she was ever comparing him with his companions, and always to his advantage. So long as a woman finds all men very much alike (as Lobelia Brewster did, save that she allowed some to be worse!), she is in no danger. But the moment in which she perceives and discriminates subtle differences, marvelling that there can be two opinions about a man's superiority, that moment the miracle has happened.

"And now I beseech thee, lady, not as though I wrote a new commandment unto thee, but that which we had from the beginning, that we love one another."

No, it could not be from Justin. She drank her tea, played with her beans abstractedly, and nibbled her slice of steaming brown bread.

"Not as though I wrote a new commandment unto thee."

No, not a new one; twelve, fifteen years old, that commandment!

"That we love one another."

Who was speaking? Who had written these words? The first letter sounded just like Mrs. Emerson, who had said she was a very poor correspondent, but that she should just "drop down" on Nancy one of these days; but this second letter never came from Mrs. Emerson.—Well, there would be an explanation some time; a pleasant one; one to smile over, and tell 'Zekiel and repeat to the neighbours; but not an unexpected, sacred, beautiful explanation, such a one as the heart of a woman could imagine, if she were young enough and happy enough to hope.

She washed her cup and plate; replaced the uneaten beans in the brown pot, and put them away with the round loaf, folded the cloth (Lobelia Brewster said Nancy always "set out her meals as if she was entertainin' company from Portland"), closed the stove dampers, carried the lighted lamp to a safe corner shelf, and lifted 'Zekiel to his cushion on the high-backed rocker, doing all with the nice precision of long habit. Then she wrapped herself warmly, and locking the lonely little house behind her, set out to finish her work in the church.

CHAPTER V

At this precise moment Justin Peabody was eating his own beans and brown bread (articles of diet of which his Detroit landlady was lamentably ignorant) at the new tavern, not far from the meeting-house.

It would not be fair to him to say that Mrs. Burbank's letter had brought him back to Edgewood, but it had certainly accelerated his steps.

For the first six years after Justin Peabody left home, he had drifted about from place to place, saving every possible dollar of his uncertain earnings in the conscious hope that he could go back to New England and ask Nancy Wentworth to marry him. The West was prosperous and progressive, but how he yearned, in idle moments, for the grimmer and more sterile soil that had given him birth!

Then came what seemed to him a brilliant chance for a lucky turn of his savings, and he invested them in an enterprise which, wonderfully as it promised, failed within six months and left him penniless. At that moment he definitely gave up all hope, and for the next few years he put Nancy as far as possible out of his mind, in the full belief that he was acting an honourable part in refusing to drag her into his tangled and fruitless way of life. If she ever did care for him,—and he could not be sure, she was always so shy,—she must have outgrown the feeling long since, and be living happily, or at least contentedly, in her own way. He was glad in spite of himself when he heard that she had never married; but at least he hadn't it on his conscience that he had kept her single!

On the seventeenth of December, Justin, his business day over, was walking toward the dreary house in which he ate and slept. As he turned the corner, he heard one woman say to another, as they watched a man stumbling sorrowfully down the street: "Going home will be the worst of all for him—to find nobody there!" That was what going home had meant for him these ten years, but he afterward felt it strange that this thought should have struck him so forcibly on that particular day. Entering the boarding-house, he found Mrs. Burbank's letter with its Edgewood postmark on the hall table, and took it up to his room. He kindled a little fire in the air-tight stove, watching the flame creep from shavings to kindlings, from kindlings to small pine, and from small pine to the round, hardwood sticks; then when the result seemed certain, he closed the stove door and sat down to read the letter. Whereupon all manner of strange things happened in his head and heart and flesh and spirit as he sat there alone, his hands in his pockets, his feet braced against the legs of the stove.

It was a cold winter night, and the snow and sleet beat against the windows. He looked about the ugly room: at the washstand with its square of oilcloth in front and its detestable bowl and pitcher; at the rigours of his white iron bedstead, with the valley in the middle of the lumpy mattress and the darns in the rumpled pillowcases; at the dull photographs of the landlady's hideous husband and children enshrined on the mantelshelf; looked at the abomination of desolation surrounding him until his soul sickened and cried out like a child's for something more like home. It was as if a spring thaw had melted his ice-bound heart, and on the crest of a wave it was drifting out into the milder waters of some unknown sea. He could have laid his head in the kind lap of a woman and cried: "Comfort me! Give me companionship or I die!"

The wind howled in the chimney and rattled the loose window-sashes; the snow, freezing as it fell, dashed against the glass with hard, cutting little blows; at least, that is the way in which the wind and snow flattered themselves they were making existence disagreeable to Justin Peabody when he read the letter; but never were elements more mistaken.

It was a June Sunday in the boarding-house bedroom; and for that matter it was not the boarding-house bedroom at all: it was the old Orthodox church on Tory Hill in Edgewood.

The windows were wide open, and the smell of the purple clover and the humming of the bees were drifting into the sweet, wide spaces within. Justin was sitting in the end of the Peabody pew, and Nancy Wentworth was beside him; Nancy, cool and restful in her white dress; dark-haired Nancy under the shadow of her shirred muslin hat.

Rise, my soul, and stretch thy wings,
Thy better portion trace.

The melodeon gave the tune, and Nancy and he stood to sing, taking the book between them. His hand touched hers, and as the music of the hymn rose and fell, the future unrolled itself before his eyes; a future in which Nancy was his wedded wife; and the happy years stretched on and on in front of them until there was a row of little heads in the old Peabody pew, and mother and father could look proudly along the line at the young things they were bringing into the house of the Lord.

The recalling of that vision worked like magic in Justin's blood. His soul rose and stretched its wings and "traced its better portion" vividly, as he sprang to his feet and walked up and down the bedroom floor. He would get a few days' leave and go back to Edgewood for Christmas, to join, with all the old neighbours, in the service at the meeting-house; and in pursuance of this resolve, he shook his fist in the face of the landlady's husband on the mantelpiece and dared him to prevent.

He had a salary of fifty dollars a month, with some very slight prospect of an increase after January. He did not see how two persons could eat, and drink, and lodge, and dress on it in Detroit, but he proposed to give Nancy Wentworth the refusal of that magnificent future, that brilliant and tempting offer. He had exactly one hundred dollars in the bank, and sixty or seventy of them would be spent in the journeys, counting two happy, blessed fares back from Edgewood to Detroit; and if he paid only his own fare back, he would throw the price of the other into the pond behind the Wentworth house. He would drop another ten dollars into the plate on Christmas Day toward the repairs on the church; if he starved, he would do that. He was a failure. Everything his hand touched turned to naught. He looked himself full in the face, recognizing his weakness, and in this supremest moment of recognition he was a stronger man than he had been an hour before. His drooping shoulders had straightened; the restless look had gone from his eyes; his sombre face had something of repose in it, the repose of a settled purpose. He was a failure, but perhaps if he took the risks (and if Nancy would take them—but that was the trouble, women were so unselfish, they were always willing to take risks, and one ought not to let them!), perhaps he might do better in trying to make a living for two than he had in working for himself alone. He would go home, tell Nancy that he was an unlucky good-for-naught, and ask her if she would try her hand at making him over.

CHAPTER VI

These were the reasons that had brought Justin Peabody to Edgewood on the Saturday afternoon before Christmas, and had taken him to the new tavern on Tory Hill, near the Meeting-House.

Nobody recognized him at the station or noticed him at the tavern, and after his supper he put on his overcoat and started out for a walk, aimlessly hoping that he might meet a friend, or failing that, intending to call on some of his old neighbours, with the view of hearing the village news and securing some information which might help him to decide when he had better lay himself and his misfortunes at Nancy Wentworth's feet. They were pretty feet! He remembered that fact well enough under the magical influence of familiar sights and sounds and odours. He was restless, miserable, anxious, homesick—not for Detroit, but for some heretofore unimagined good; yet, like Bunyan's shepherd boy in the Valley of Humiliation, he carried "the herb called Hearts-ease in his bosom," for he was at last loving consciously.

How white the old church looked, and how green the blinds! It must have been painted very lately: that meant that the parish was fairly prosperous. There were new shutters in the belfry tower, too; he remembered the former open space and the rusty bell, and he liked the change. Did the chimney use to be in that corner? No; but his father had always said it would have drawn better if it had been put there in the beginning. New shingles within a year: that was evident to a practised eye. He wondered if anything had been done to the inside of the building, but he must wait until the morrow to see, for, of course, the doors would be locked. No; the one at the right side was ajar. He opened it softly and stepped into the tiny square entry that he recalled so well—the one through which the Sunday-school children ran out to the steps from their catechism, apparently enjoying the sunshine after a spell of orthodoxy; the little entry where the village girls congregated while waiting for the last bell to ring—they made a soft blur of pink and blue and buff, a little flutter of curls and braids and fans and sunshades, in his mind's eye, as he closed the outer door behind him and gently opened the inner one. The church was flooded with moonlight and snowlight, and there was one lamp burning at the back of the pulpit; a candle, too, on the pulpit steps. There was the tip-tap-tip of a tack-hammer going on in a distant corner. Was somebody hanging Christmas garlands? The new red carpet attracted his notice, and as he grew accustomed to the dim light, it carried his eye along the aisle he had trod so many years of Sundays, to the old familiar pew. The sound of the hammer ceased and a woman rose from her knees. A stranger was doing for the family honour what he ought himself to have done. The woman turned to shake her skirt, and it was Nancy Wentworth. He might have known it. Women were always faithful; they always remembered old landmarks, old days, old friends, old duties. His father and mother and Esther were all gone; who but dear Nancy would have made the old Peabody pew right and tidy for the Christmas festival? Bless her kind womanly heart!

She looked just the same to him as when he last saw her. Mercifully he seemed to have held in remembrance all these years not so much her youthful bloom as her general qualities of mind and heart: her cheeriness, her spirit, her unflagging zeal, her bright womanliness. Her grey dress was turned up in front over a crimson moreen petticoat. She had on a cosy jacket, a fur turban of some sort with a redbreast in it, and her cheeks were flushed from exertion. “Sweet records, and promises as sweet,” had always met in Nancy’s face, and either he had forgotten how pretty she was, or else she had absolutely grown prettier during his absence.

Nancy would have chosen the supreme moment of meeting very differently, but she might well have chosen worse. She unpinned her skirt and brushed the threads off, smoothed the pew cushions carefully, and took a last stitch in the ragged hassock. She then lifted the Bible and the hymn-book from the rack, and putting down a bit of flannel on the pulpit steps, took a flatiron from an oil-stove, and opening the ancient books, pressed out the well-thumbed leaves one by one with infinite care. After replacing the volumes in their accustomed place, she first extinguished the flame of her stove, which she tucked out of sight, and then blew out the lamp and the candle. The church was still light enough for objects to be seen in a shadowy way, like the objects in a dream, and Justin did not realize that he was a man in the flesh, looking at a woman; spying, it might be, upon her privacy. He was one part of a dream and she another, and he stood as if waiting, and fearing, to be awakened.

Nancy, having done all, came out of the pew, and standing in the aisle, looked back at the scene of her labours with pride and content. And as she looked, some desire to stay a little longer in the dear old place must have come over her, or some dread of going back to her lonely cottage, for she sat down in Justin’s corner of the pew with folded hands, her eyes fixed dreamily on the pulpit and her ears hearing: “Not as though I wrote a new commandment unto thee, but that which we had from the beginning.”

Justin's grasp on the latch tightened as he prepared to close the door and leave the place, but his instinct did not warn him quickly enough, after all, for, obeying some uncontrollable impulse, Nancy suddenly fell on her knees in the pew and buried her face in the cushions.

The dream broke, and in an instant Justin was a man—worse than that, he was an eavesdropper, ashamed of his unsuspected presence. He felt himself standing, with covered head and feet shod, in the holy temple of a woman's heart.

But his involuntary irreverence brought abundant grace with it. The glimpse and the revelation wrought their miracles silently and irresistibly, not by the slow processes of growth which Nature demands for her enterprises, but with the sudden swiftness of the spirit. In an instant changes had taken place in Justin's soul which his so-called "experiencing religion" twenty-five years back had been powerless to effect. He had indeed been baptized then, but the recording angel could have borne witness that this second baptism fructified the first, and became the real herald of the new birth and the new creature.

CHAPTER VII

Justin Peabody silently closed the inner door, and stood in the entry with his head bent and his heart in a whirl until he should hear Nancy rise to her feet. He must take this Heaven-sent chance of telling her all, but how do it without alarming her?

A moment, and her step sounded in the stillness of the empty church.

Obeying the first impulse, he passed through the outer door, and standing on the step, knocked once, twice, three times; then, opening it a little and speaking through the chink, he called, "Is Miss Nancy Wentworth here?"

"I'm here!" in a moment came Nancy's answer, and then, with a little wondering tremor in her voice, as if a hint of the truth had already dawned: "What's wanted?"

"You're wanted, Nancy, wanted badly, by Justin Peabody, come back from the West."

The door opened wide, and Justin faced Nancy standing half-way down the aisle, her eyes brilliant, her lips parted. A week ago Justin's apparition confronting her in the empty Meeting-House after nightfall, even had she been prepared for it as now, by his voice, would have terrified her beyond measure. Now it seemed almost natural and inevitable. She had spent these last days in the church where both of them had been young and happy together; the two letters had brought him vividly to mind, and her labour in the old Peabody pew had been one long excursion into the past in which he was the most prominent and the best-loved figure.

"I said I'd come back to you when my luck turned, Nancy."

These were so precisely the words she expected him to say, should she ever see him again face to face, that for an additional moment they but heightened her sense of unreality.

"Well, the luck hasn't turned, after all, but I couldn't wait any longer. Have you given a thought to me all these years, Nancy?"

“More than one, Justin”; for the very look upon his face, the tenderness of his voice, the attitude of his body, outran his words and told her what he had come home to say, told her that her years of waiting were over at last.

“You ought to despise me for coming back again with only myself and my empty hands to offer you.”

How easy it was to speak his heart out in this dim and quiet place! How tongue-tied he would have been, sitting on the black haircloth sofa in the Wentworth parlour and gazing at the open soapstone stove!

“Oh, men are such fools!” cried Nancy, smiles and tears struggling together in her speech, as she sat down suddenly in her own pew and put her hands over her face.

“They are,” agreed Justin humbly, “but I’ve never stopped loving you, whenever I’ve had time for thinking or loving. And I wasn’t sure that you really cared anything about me; and how could I have asked you when I hadn’t a dollar in the world?”

“There are other things to give a woman besides dollars, Justin.”

“Are there? Well, you shall have them all, every one of them, Nancy, if you can make up your mind to do without the dollars; for dollars seem to be just what I can’t manage.”

Her hand was in his by this time, and they were sitting side by side in the cushionless, carpetless Wentworth pew. The door stood open; the winter moon shone in upon them. That it was beginning to grow cold in the church passed unnoticed. The grasp of the woman’s hand seemed to give the man new hope and courage, and Justin’s warm, confiding, pleading pressure brought balm to Nancy, balm and healing for the wounds her pride had suffered; joy, too, half-conscious still, that her life need not be lived to the end in unfruitful solitude. She had waited, “as some grey lake lies, full and smooth, awaiting the star below the twilight.” Justin Peabody might have been no other woman’s star, but he was Nancy’s!

“Just you sitting beside me here makes me feel as if I’d been asleep or dead all these years, and just born over again,” said Justin. “I’ve led a respectable, hard-working, honest life, Nancy,” he continued, “and I don’t owe any man a cent; the trouble is that no man owes me one. I've got enough money to pay two fares back to Detroit on Monday, although I was terribly afraid you wouldn't let me do it. It'll need a good deal of thinking and planning, Nancy, for we shall be very poor."

Nancy had been storing up fidelity and affection deep, deep in the hive of her heart all these years, and now the honey of her helpfulness stood ready to be gathered.

"Could I keep hens in Detroit?" she asked. "I can always make them pay."

"Hens—in three rooms, Nancy?"

Her face fell. "And no yard?"

"No yard."

A moment's pause, and then the smile came. "Oh, well, I've had yards and hens for thirty-five years. Doing without them will be a change. I can take in sewing."

"No, you can't, Nancy. I need your backbone and wits and pluck and ingenuity, but if I can't ask you to sit with your hands folded for the rest of your life, as I'd like to, you shan't use them for other people. You're marrying me to make a man of me, but I'm not marrying you to make you a drudge."

His voice rang clear and true in the silence, and Nancy's heart vibrated at the sound.

"Oh, Justin, Justin!" she whispered. "There's something wrong somewhere, but we'll find it out together, you and I, and make it right. You're not like a failure. You don't even look poor, Justin; there isn't a man in Edgewood to compare with you, or I should be washing his dishes and darning his stockings this minute. And I am not a pauper! There'll be the rent of my little house and a carload of my furniture, so you can put the three-room idea out of your mind, and your firm will offer you a larger salary when you tell them you have a wife to take care of. Oh, I see it all, and it is as easy and bright and happy as can be!"

Justin put his arm around her and drew her close, with such a throb of gratitude for her belief and trust that it moved him almost to tears.

There was a long pause: then he said:—

“Now I shall call for you to-morrow morning after the last bell has stopped ringing, and we will walk up the aisle together and sit in the old Peabody pew. We shall be a nine-days’ wonder anyway, but this will be equal to an announcement, especially if you take my arm. We don’t either of us like to be stared at, but this will show without a word what we think of each other and what we’ve promised to be to each other, and it’s the only thing that will make me feel sure of you and settled in my mind after all these mistaken years. Have you got the courage, Nancy?”

“I shouldn’t wonder! I guess if I’ve had courage enough to wait for you, I’ve got courage enough to walk up the aisle with you and marry you besides!” said Nancy.—“Now it is too late for us to stay here any longer, and you must see me only as far as my gate, for perhaps you haven’t forgotten yet how interested the Brewsters are in their neighbours.”

They stood at the little Wentworth gate for a moment, hand close clasped in hand. The night was clear, the air was cold and sparkling, but with nothing of bitterness in it; the sky was steely blue and the evening star glowed and burned like a tiny sun. Nancy remembered the shepherd’s song she had taught the Sunday-school children, and repeated softly:—

For I my sheep was watching
Beneath the silent skies,
When sudden, far to eastward,
I saw a star arise;
Then all the peaceful heavens
With sweetest music rang,
And glory, glory, glory!
The happy angels sang.

So I this night am joyful,
Though I can scarce tell why,
It seemeth me that glory
Hath met us very nigh;
And we, though poor and humble,

Have part in heavenly plan,
For, born to-night, the Prince of Peace
Shall rule the heart of man.

Justin's heart melted within him like wax to the woman's vision and the woman's touch.

"Oh, Nancy, Nancy!" he whispered. "If I had brought my bad luck to you long, long ago, would you have taken me then, and have I lost years of such happiness as this?"

"There are some things it is not best for a man to be certain about," said Nancy, with a wise smile and a last good-night.

CHAPTER VIII

"Ring out, sweet bells,
O'er woods and dells
Your lovely strains repeat,
While happy throngs
With joyous songs
Each accent gladly greet."

Christmas morning in the old Tory Hill Meeting-House was felt by all of the persons who were present in that particular year to be a most exciting and memorable occasion.

The old sexton quite outdid himself, for although he had rung the bell for more than thirty years, he had never felt greater pride or joy in his task. Was not his son John home for Christmas, and John's wife, and a grandchild newly named Nathaniel for himself? Were there not spareribs and turkeys and cranberries and mince pies on the pantry shelves, and barrels of rosy Baldwins in the cellar and bottles of mother's root beer just waiting to give a holiday pop? The bell itself forgot its age and the suspicion of a crack that dulled its voice on a damp day, and, inspired by the bright, frosty air, the sexton's inspiring pull, and the Christmas spirit, gave out nothing but joyous tones.

Ding-dong! Ding-dong! It fired the ambitions of star scholars about to recite hymns and sing solos. It thrilled little girls expecting dolls before night. It excited beyond bearing dozens of little boys being buttoned into refractory overcoats. Ding-dong! Ding-dong! Mothers' fingers trembled when they heard it, and mothers' voices cried: "If that is the second bell, the children will never be ready in time! Where are the overshoes? Where are the mittens? Hurry, Jack! Hurry, Jennie!" Ding-dong! Ding-dong! "Where's Sally's muff? Where's father's fur cap? Is the sleigh at the door? Are the hot soapstones in? Have all of you your money for the contribution box?"

Ding-dong! Ding-dong! It was a blithe bell, a sweet, true bell, a holy bell, and to Justin, pacing his tavern room, as to Nancy, trembling in her maiden chamber, it rang a Christmas message:—

Awake, glad heart! Arise and sing;
It is the birthday of thy King!

The congregation filled every seat in the old Meeting-House.

As Maria Sharp had prophesied, there was one ill-natured spinster from a rival village who declared that the church floor looked like Joseph's coat laid out smooth; but in the general chorus of admiration, approval, and good will, this envious speech, though repeated from mouth to mouth, left no sting.

Another item of interest long recalled was the fact that on that august and unapproachable day the pulpit vases stood erect and empty, though Nancy Wentworth had filled them every Sunday since any one could remember. This instance, though felt at the time to be of mysterious significance if the cause were ever revealed, paled into nothingness when, after the ringing of the last bell, Nancy Wentworth walked up the aisle on Justin Peabody's arm, and they took their seats side by side in the old family pew.

("And consid'able close, too, though there was plenty o' room!")

("And no one that I ever heard of so much as suspicioned that they had ever kept company!")

("And do you s'pose she knew Justin was expected back when she scrubbed his pew a-Friday?")

("And this explains the empty pulpit vases!")

("And I always said that Nancy would make a real handsome couple if she ever got anybody to couple with!")

During the unexpected and solemn procession of the two up the aisle the soprano of the village choir stopped short in the middle of the Doxology, and the three other voices carried it to the end without any treble. Also, among those present there were some who could not remember afterward the precise petitions wafted upward in the opening prayer.

And could it be explained otherwise than by cheerfully acknowledging the bounty of an overruling Providence that Nancy Wentworth should have had a new winter dress for the first time in five years—a winter dress of dark brown cloth to match her beaver muff and victorine? The existence of this toilette had been known and discussed in Edgewood for a month past, and it was thought to be nothing more than a proper token of respect from a member of the carpet committee to the general magnificence of the church on the occasion of its reopening after repairs. Indeed, you could have identified every member of the Dorcas Society that Sunday morning by the freshness of her apparel. The brown dress, then, was generally expected; but why the white cashmere waist with collar and cuffs of point lace, devised only and suitable only for the minister's wedding, where it first saw the light?

"The white waist can only be explained as showing distinct hope!" whispered the minister's wife during the reading of the church notices.

"To me it shows more than hope; I am very sure that Nancy would never take any wear out of that lace for hope; it means certainty!" answered Maria, who was always strong in the prophetic line.

By sermon time Justin's identity had dawned upon most of the congregation. A stranger to all but one or two at first, his presence in the Peabody pew brought his face and figure back, little by little, to the minds of the old parishioners.

When the contribution plate was passed, the sexton always began at the right-wing pews, as all the sextons before him had done for a hundred years. Every eye in the church was already turned upon Justin and Nancy, and it was with almost a gasp that those in the vicinity saw a ten dollar bill fall in the plate. The sexton reeled, or, if that is too intemperate a word for a pillar of the church, the good man tottered, but caught hold of the pew rail with one hand, and, putting the thumb of his other over the bill, proceeded quickly to the next pew, lest the stranger should think better of his gift, or demand change, as had occasionally been done in the olden time.

Nancy never fluttered an eyelash, but sat quietly by Justin's side with her bosom rising and falling under the beaver fur and her cold hands clasped tight in the little brown muff. Far from grudging this appreciable part of their slender resources, she thrilled with pride to see Justin's offering fall in the plate.

Justin was too absorbed in his own thoughts to notice anything, but his munificent contribution had a most unexpected effect upon his reputation, after all; for on that day, and on many another later one, when his sudden marriage and departure with Nancy Wentworth were under discussion, the neighbours said to one another:—

"Justin must be making money fast out West! He put ten dollars in the contribution plate a-Sunday, and paid the minister ten more next day for marryin' him to Nancy; so the Peabody luck has turned at last!" which, as a matter of fact, it had.

"And all the time," said the chairman of the carpet committee to the treasurer of the Dorcas Society—"all the time, little as she realized it, Nancy was laying the carpet in her own pew. Now she's married to Justin she'll be the makin' of him, or I miss my guess. You can't do a thing with men folks without they're right alongside where you can keep your eye and hand on 'em. Justin's handsome and good and stiddy; all he need is some nice woman to put starch into him. The Edgewood Peabodys never had a mite o' stiffenin' in 'em,—limp as dishrags, every blessed one! Nancy Wentworth fairly rustles with starch. Justin hadn't been engaged to her but a few hours when they walked up the aisle together, but did you notice the way he carried his head? I declare I thought 't would fall off behind! I shouldn't wonder a mite but they prospered and come back every summer to set in the old Peabody Pew."

Milton Keynes UK
Ingram Content Group UK Ltd.
UKHW050641101123
432322UK00016B/631